"Your words touched my h
what I'm going through righ

Greg Parker, online reader

"I just read your latest newsletter article. It was awesome! Thanks for the tap of Knowledge from God!"

Jan Dickerson, On Our Journey Home subscriber

"I printed out the Newsletter page that you did on the Holy Spirit a while back, and it remains in my prayer book as a constant reminder. Bless you."

Doug, On Our Journey Home subscriber

"Staci has planted a seed deep in my soul and has challenged me to grow, love and be myself. There is no doubt about her unending love for Christ. It shows in her words, her actions and in her heart. In a few short months, Staci has opened a whole new world for me. In reading her articles, I can laugh, cry and rejoice because for certain they are real and very much inspiring."

Betty Aragon, reader

"I just had to let you know,......*I love everything that I've read on your site!* God never changes and His laws and love are forever. You have confirmed this in fulfilling your calling to 'tell it like it is' (even many pastors and teachers have let this generation of young people down by compromising). I will just keep on keeping on with my 'ol fogey ideas thanks to wonderful ones like you that God uses to let me know that ... morals, purity, integrity, character and holiness are forever right up to date."

Ruby Younce, online reader

"I just read the article you wrote in the Heartlight Magazine. It really touched me. The article gave me some encouragement that I needed. Thank you so much. I will continue to press towards the mark that Christ wants me to live in my life--to live for him and show HIS love to others."

Tracy A Hicks, online reader

"The first time I read a work by Staci Stallings I was struck by how relatable her writing is. Uplifting and encouraging, but more importantly, expressing the feelings we all have but few of us can find the words for as she does. Buy two copies of 'Reflections on Life.' One for you, and one for your best friend, who will be forever thankful."

Vic Johnson, Founder of MyDailyInsights.com

"Thanks for a well written piece on an extraordinary subject. In infects us all. We all want to be recognized as a person of value. Unfortunately, many were raised in a 'none' encouraging environment. It seems that even after redemption through Christ, many still only find their value in being 'worldly' significant. Thanks again for your work."

Steve Barack, online reader

"Staci Stallings' upbeat articles are the perfect vehicle for enhancing a positive attitude. Reading Staci's articles offers respite and that necessary support and encouragement. Staci makes this world a nicer place to be."

Jane Mullikin, Spiritual Sisters, Online Ezine

"Staci's writings will sometimes make you laugh and sometimes make you cry, but they will always leave you feeling good inside. Time spent reading Staci's writings is time well spent."

Danny Woodall, On Our Journey Home subscriber

Afterward

If the messages in **Reflections on Life** blessed you, please consider letting us know.

You can email Staci at:

staci_stallings@hotmail.com

Also, you can check out Staci's website and newsletter at:

www.stacistallings.com

Staci's newsletter, **On Our Journey Home** is sent out monthly and contains Staci's newest articles, insights, quotes, inspiration, news, and book releases. You can subscribe by sending a blank email to:

newsletter@stacistallings.com

Remember, Staci's books aren't in any store—although you can special order them from your local bookstore. The easiest way to get them is straight from the website.

www.stacistallings.com

Check it out today…

You'll feel better for the experience!

About the Author

A stay-at-home mom with a husband, three kids and a writing addiction on the side, Staci Stallings has seen two Inspirational Romance novels in print, "The Long Way Home" and "Eternity." Stallings has also been a featured writer in the "From the Heart" series, in "Chicken Soup for the Body and Soul," "Soul Matters," and in numerous inspirational, spiritual, and family-oriented ezines across the Internet. Although she lives in Amarillo, Texas and her main career right now is her family, Staci touches thousands of lives across the globe every month with her newsletter, "On Our Journey Home," which is featured at her website, www.stacistallings.com Come on over for a visit. You'll feel better for the experience!

Reflections on Life

Staci Stallings

Copyright © Staci Stallings, 2005

Published by:
Spirit Light Publishing
Amarillo, TX,
through lulu.com

Printed in the United States of America

Cover Design, KDJ Outsourcing
design@kdjoutsourcing.com

Library of Congress Cataloging-in-Publication Data
is available upon request.

ISBN 1-4116-5877-9

To those who have inspired me along my faith journey—my family, my friends, and all those who have inspired me from afar and from a-near. For the songs, the books, the quotes, the messages, the conversations, and the talents you have given to the world, which continue to challenge me to live this life to the fullest. I will never be able to repay you on this side of Heaven. My only hope is that when we get to the other side, in the eternities to come we will have a chance to sit down and compare notes.

Just so you know, I love you all!

Contents

When you live a life of love,
Time becomes meaningless,
Limits are removed,
And you just want to
Open your heart a little wider.

--Staci Stallings

Foreword

I did not set out to write a book of reflections. At first these stories were meant only as a marketing tool. My publisher said I needed three articles so they could use them in marketing. I complied but soon realized if anyone was going to "market" them, it was going to have to be me. So, I began submitting them to various places. As the archive of articles grew, the places they were published grew as well.

Then about eight months ago, I started noticing that I had stopped using them to market and started using them just to capture thoughts, feelings, reflections that the Holy Spirit was flooding through my life. I can't really explain how this happens for I don't even understand it myself, but things will happen in life, and the underlying spiritual meaning slowly becomes clear to me. The lessons are *everywhere.*

They are in music—Christian and secular. They are in nature and my contact with others. They are in books and movies. They are in events and small moments that usually pass by unseen. As I began to capture these lessons into words, the floodgates opened. Even though I knew I had no time to use all of these articles to market, that became a secondary consideration, if a consideration at all. I simply didn't want to forget what He was telling me.

A few days ago someone very special to me asked for recommendations for things to read. I thought of my articles, and I wanted a way to hand them to him. That's how this book was born. At the end of each article, I have placed the year it was created because they are not organized in chronological order in the book as to when each was created. This date stamp is not important to anyone other than me, but I hope you will indulge me this small reminder for my own benefit.

I pray that these simple thoughts will bless you as much as they have blessed me! May your journey be filled with lessons of life, love, faith, and hope. God bless you forever.

Staci Stallings

1

On Living With Christ

I can do all things through Christ who strengthens me.

-Philippians 4:13

It's Not Up to You

The ego in us tells us that *we* have to do it—whatever "it" happens to be. It may be working or finding work, or studying or practicing, or learning an instrument or learning anything. "It" could be a lot of things, but the biggest lie in this life is that "it" is up to us to do.

In the book "Grace Rules" by Steve McVey, Mr. McVey leads with an interesting scenario of Jesus waking up in the morning and deciding what He was going to do for God today. In the story, Jesus decides that it would be a good thing to do a few miracles because that would get some attention, and casting out some demons might also be a good attention getter. The essence of what Mr. McVey was trying to say is that if we look to Jesus for our example, then our "planning" our day is completely ridiculous.

After reading Mr. McVey's first book "Grace Walk," I realized I'd been doing exactly that. I had yellow notebooks filled with to-do lists. As I looked back on them, they were always the same thing with only a few variations. Pay bills, write article, work on website, work on book, etc. Over and over until you would've thought I had it memorized. There were also things on those lists that I didn't get to, things that had never been crossed out.

I told a friend of mine after seeing what I had been doing that I now understood why I was always so frustrated. If I put ten things on the list in the morning, inevitably by two, there were five more things to add. By the time I quit at six, I had added another six or eight things. So in addition to not getting all of the things I had written down at the first of the day done, now I had 14 more things to do. It was like I was on a squirrel wheel going round and round and round. Sure I had good intentions of doing what I was doing for God. I even put things in His hands when they seemed overwhelming, but it never occurred to me to put the whole day in His hands and let Him decide what we were going to do.

The first day I did that was the most empowering day of my life. For years I had worked to position myself as someone who could help other authors with marketing. It never worked. It was as if no one else cared about marketing, which of course is completely ridiculous, but that's the way it felt.

Then that day, I let go and let God. In the course of about five hours suddenly people were asking my opinion on these matters from so many different directions I could hardly keep up, but of course, I didn't have to. During that day my email program totally shut down twice. Most days I would've been freaking out. That day, I said, "Okay, God, then what am I supposed to do?"

Instantly a thought would come to me. That day—in one day—I helped four different people with their marketing, replied to every email that came my way, exercised, vacuumed my kitchen, sent in my tax information, wrote letters and got them mailed, played with my kids in the backyard, sent my newsletter out, read for 30 minutes, listened to a tape, took my kids to school, went and picked them up from school… It was as if I would think of it, and it would do itself.

And the cool thing is, it continues to be that way. I've been "redirected" many times. In fact this article is a redirect because what I was going to work on, I couldn't find. So let God decide your "it," and let Him decide when and how that will look. In short, realize it's not up to you. Instead let Him do the "its" He has planned for your life through you today. You will be amazed. (2005)

Who Has He Helped Through You Today?

As I write this, it is December 5th. I mention that because with Christmas coming up, it is the season of giving. Along with the normal gifts, this is also the season when our thoughts turn to those less fortunate.

The paper angel trees go up in the malls. The kettles and bells come out. The requests from organizations that help the needy – from food banks to Toys-for-Tots – rise exponentially.

This is also the time our thoughts take in all the things we are grateful for and all the things that we wish for in the coming year. In short, this is a very special time of the year.

As January approaches, my thoughts have been on the New Years Resolution I made last year. The resolution itself was simple – to be an angel to as many people as possible. At the time I couldn't have foreseen many of the opportunities that came my way. In fact, maybe I thought of it more as a wish than a real resolution.

However, God used that desire to show me things about life I had never seen before, like how little it takes to make a difference, how a simple heartfelt note can change someone forever, how easy it is to love when you put fear out of the equation.

As the year progressed, I learned what it means to let Him help others through me. I learned that I don't have to do it. All I have to do is let Him guide my heart and my hands. All I have to do is let Him do it through me.

God has helped countless people through me this year – the homeless lady who desperately needed work and who now cleans my house (praise God for her!), the homeless people three states away who are wearing something I no longer needed, the young mother struggling through a heartbreaking betrayal who received a book and a CD filled with Christ's love for her and her family and knew someone cared.

The opportunities were boundless—as they always are. The biggest problem is we find so many ways to talk ourselves out of helping. We're too busy. It takes too long. It costs too much. We have our own problems.

The real problem is that the focus of all of those excuses is in the wrong direction – on "I" instead of on "Him".

St. Theresa once said that we are the only hands that Jesus has on this earth, the only feet Jesus has on this earth now. He wants to use our lives, to work through us in the world.

As the words of a song by Keith Urban that's just come into my life says: "Days go by. . . it's all we've been given, so we better start living right now, 'cause days go by."

I don't think I'm going to set any goals this coming year as I have in the past. I think this year my resolution will be simply to let Him work through me every single day. And my question at the end of each day will be simply, "Who has He helped through me today?"

If you are thinking of trying out my "angel resolution" in your life – even if it is April or August or October when you read this – I know for a fact that you are one more person I can say "This is someone He has helped through me today."

Peace and joy in your new life as it starts today, because if you take this challenge, today really is the first day of a brand new life. (2004)

The Gifts

Since reading Brennan Manning's *The Ragamuffin Gospel,* the meaning of the gifts of the Holy Spirit has suddenly come alive for me. Prior to reading about how grace can transform your life, I was already pretty solid in "letting Him do it." As a reformed control-freak, I had made a conscious choice to stop trying to control everything. I took my hands off the wheel and said, "God, You take my life where You want it to go."

It didn't take long before I could see how much better He put things together in my life. I could see how He put the people I most needed in my life, how He arranged meetings and "coincidences" to guide me in where I was supposed to go, how He formed a relationship seemingly for one purpose even though He had something much bigger in mind. However, it wasn't until Manning's book that I understood that the Holy Spirit was not "out there." It was "in here." In me.

It was literally God's Spirit in my heart, in my body, in my spirit. Wow! Did that understanding open doors!

I had always been taught about the gifts of the Holy Spirit—wisdom, knowledge, understanding, fortitude, right judgment, fear of the Lord, and piety. However, after letting the Holy Spirit not just direct my paths but begin to live through me, I have come to really understand these gifts in a new light.

A friend of mine is teaching a 7th grade Sunday school class. She came one day depressed because during the past Sunday's class her personal life had interfered with her teaching life. She said, "I just think I failed them." I then asked her if she had put it in the Holy Spirit's hands. "Yes." To which, I asked, "Do you think the Holy Spirit can fail?" A long pause. "No."

"Then if you've put the situation in the Holy Spirit's hands, if He is living through you, and the Holy Spirit can't fail, then can you fail?"

It was the first time I had ever put it in those words even for myself, but at that moment, I got it. The more I put my life in His hands and let Him take control in situations instead of me trying to control them based on my meager knowledge and understanding, the more I see that nothing is impossible. Even if something looks like a failure to me, He has a plan.

When you let go and let the Holy Spirit take control, no longer will you have "I should've said but I didn't" or "I would've, but I was afraid." When He speaks to your heart, you learn to listen and to do and to say. Better than that you begin to let HIM listen and do and say through you, and when that happens, the gifts that follow are more amazing than you can ever imagine! (2004)

Stage or Altar

Plastic Christians. You know the kind. They know all the words, spout all the rules, sing all the songs, join everything, and they look really good doing it, too. Their suits are pressed. Their ties are straight. Their dresses are the mint of modesty. And yet, it all seems too good, too perfect. All plastic, no feeling.

Recently I came face-to-face with the plastic Christian in me. Oh, she talked a good game. To the world, she looked good in her deeds. She was no doubt Christian, but plastic nonetheless.

You see, deeds done out of fear of being found less than the perfect Christian are dead deeds—no matter how good they look. A song I heard by Casting Crowns called, "Stained Glass Masquerade" puts it this way:

"Am I the only one that's traded in the altar for a stage?"

Now before you jump on the bandwagon of spirit-bashing the choir or the readers or those in other visible ministries, I suggest as Jesus said, that you look first at yourself. If you are without sin here, then you may cast a stone.

These words are not talking only about the more visible ministries in the church. They are talking about you and your walk everyday with Christ. Is it a performance or a sacrifice? Are you on the stage or on the altar?

If you're not sure, from experience, ministry of performance looks like this: you say all the right words, but your heart feels none of them. You read the Bible religiously, go to church without fail, you can recite all the rules and the prayers as well—but it all feels empty as if you are going through all the motions because that's what's expected. You join the organizations, help with the youth, volunteer for every fundraiser, attend classes, teach classes. You serve and serve and serve until you've got no more to give, and then you find a way to give some more. You feel burned out and used up, and yet there are still people hurting, still more you should give. You want to live out the Christian life, but the reality for you is, it's tiring work.

That's performance. Performance is going on your own ability, choosing the Tree of the Knowledge of Good and Evil over resting in the Tree of Life.

Things look and feel very different when you're on the altar. When you're on the altar, the comprehension of your smallness when compared with His enormity is reassuring—not judgmental, frightening, and depressing. You suddenly realize you can't, but He can. That understanding frees you to jump into situations where failure is a real possibility, but even if you fail by the world's standards in the task He whispered on your heart, you know that somehow from His perspective, even that failure is a victory. Better, you trust that it's a victory and move forward in confidence—not because you think you can do it, but because you know you don't have to—He will.

On the altar when you read the Bible, you read it because it's fascinating, because you hear Him speaking to you—not because you have to or because you're supposed to. Prayers might be memorized or they might well be, "Hey, God. It's me, so glad You're here."

On the altar, you let go of the driving need to prove anything to anybody. You just are. You open your life to Him, just as a sacrificed animal on the altar is cut open, so are you. In a very real way, you die to who you were, to your own ability, to your own performance. Impressing others pales in comparison with being real and being honest about your fears, about your failures, and about who you really are. You suddenly have no desire to wear the mask of plastic Christianity, and the more your mask is stripped away by His loving, accepting presence, the more you begin to allow others in your presence to remove theirs.

As I thought about the concept of stage or altar, performance or sacrifice, the story of Cain and Abel slid into my consciousness. Has there ever been a more perfect example of what performance-based Christianity leads to?

There's Cain tilling his little performance heart out, thinking how pleased God is going to be with this offering and being pretty pleased with his offering before it even gets to God. How could God not be impressed? After all, Cain reserved the best of his harvest for the Lord. But when he presents the offering to God, God shrugs. Instantly Cain gets angry. How dare the Lord not fawn over his offering!

Then, in walks Abel who presents his offering to the Lord. Abel, innocent and trusting, a sacrifice personified. And the Lord is pleased with Abel's gift. This infuriates Cain who rises up, and in his jealousy and anger, kills his brother.

Are you Cain in your Christian walk? Do you look around and become envious of someone else's service, of someone else's gifts? Do you judge those who aren't "as Christian" as they "should be"? Are you completely sure that God will accept your gifts over someone else's because yours are so obviously better? Do you work for God, or does God work through you?

Take it from someone who was on that stage for far too long: It's a lonely, miserable, rotten place to be. More over, as scary as being on the altar sounds, the freedom it affords is worth every spotlight you have to give up.

So, are you on the stage or the altar? (2005)

There's Gotta Be An Easier Way

Have you ever had a dream that was so close you could nearly reach out and touch it? And yet every time you put your hand out, it turns out to be a mirage. You work and work. You put your all into making the dream come to fruition, but when you get to the place where you think you want to be, all you find is more work to do.

I see it with the two college students who work for me and are always hanging out at my house. It seems like they work and work, and yet graduation feels no closer. I see it in my carpenter husband. He stresses out when a job is finishing up because "what are we going to do next?" But he also stresses out when the job is going because "how are we going to get this all done?"

I see it in my own life. I set up meetings to talk with people about my books. The meetings always go well—some even go really well. But then, the sales don't come through like I thought they would (read: hoped they would). It's not that God's not on my side. I know for a fact He is because I've seen His hand at work in too many areas of my life to doubt it. Yet I'm still left wondering, why does it have to be this hard?

In thinking about this phenomenon, I suddenly realized that this very feeling is encapsulated in the scene at Gethsemane. Christ is kneeling, praying, and He says, "Father, if it's possible, let this cup pass Me by..." What He's really saying is, "God, listen, please, there's got to be an easier way." He knows what is coming. He knows to the bottom of His soul this is not going to be fun. In fact, I think He's not even totally sure He can pull it off.

Think about it. He's been asked, nae, sent, to save the whole world. That's not exactly a miniscule assignment. On top of that, He knows that in order to accomplish this, He will have to suffer and die—on a cross, beaten bloody, and humiliated. That's not exactly the most comforting thought in the world.

And so, He asks God one more time if this plan was really necessary. Apparently the answer was, "Yes, it's necessary." In my mind I can see Jesus say, "Well, okay then." He stands up and walks forward into His future.

Here's the thing though, while we're in "hard," it's tempting to give up. It's tempting to say, "This isn't worth it" and walk away from God's ultimate dream for us. But if we do... if we walk away because it's too hard, we will miss the glorious resurrection day. We will miss that day on which God takes our dream, molds it into His vision and releases it to the world in a burst of golden light.

Sure, it could be easier, but then the triumph of our Easter Sunday wouldn't be met with such rejoicing. And who knows, if we didn't go through our Good Friday, Easter might never come at all. (2003)

There is No "For"

When I was in my dad's choir in high school and college, I was the lead musician and singer for years. There was one point in the Mass that being the leader, I really had to be on my toes or a whole church-full of people would get totally confused.

The prayer that precedes this moment goes like this:

"Through Him, with Him, and in Him, in the unity of the Holy Spirit. All glory and honor is Yours, Almighty Father, forever and ever."

To which the congregation is to respond, "Amen." It's called the Great Amen. It's called that for a reason that we will get to in a moment. But from the lead choir person's perspective, this is a moment of great peril—especially if the priest can't sing.

You see, if this prayer is spoken, a spoken "Amen" flows almost without a breath. So, to jump in with music, you have to be ready. Over the years I trained myself to get really good at listening for this prayer which comes at the end of a much longer prayer. That longer prayer makes it that much easier to get distracted and miss your tiny window of opportunity.

Eventually, I took to saying that prayer under my breath so I wouldn't miss it. Doing so, it became ingrained in my brain—deeply. However, it wasn't until recently that I even understood what it really means.

I received an email from a lady who had Googled "Abide in Me" and found my article by the same name. She wrote and suggested that I get the book "Grace Walk" by Steven McVey, which I did.

In the beginning of this excellent book, Mr. McVey talks about how after we get saved, we think we must then get to work *for God*. We throw ourselves into that effort—joining church organizations, reading the Bible, praying, studying, evangelizing… But at the end of all of our efforts, we come to a place where we just aren't happy or fulfilled or particularly joyful. We are depleted and tired. Stressed out and a little resentful. And in all honesty, we don't really see the point of all this effort.

Of course as good Christians, we soon feel really far away from God, so we redouble our efforts for Him and go back to work.

However, like Martha in the story of Martha and Mary, we get angry. Eventually we turn to Jesus and like Martha and say, "Why don't you see all the stuff I'm doing for You?" When Jesus looked at Martha and said, "Mary has chosen the better part to sit at my feet and just be with me," Martha's response is ours. "But that's not doing anything for You. That's just sitting there!"

Mr. McVey points out something interesting. He says if Jesus had asked Mary for a cup of water, do you not think she would've jumped up to get it? Of course, she would have. But He didn't ask her because His only goal was to be with her and to have her want to be with Him. That's it.

As I thought about this concept, the words of that prayer long-ago memorized came to mind:

"Through Him, with Him, in Him, in the unity of the Holy Spirit All glory and honor is Yours, Almighty Father, forever and ever."

Read it again, and this time, notice there is not a "for" anywhere in there. It simply asks us to be in a relationship through Him, with Him, and in Him. If we do that, I am convinced that the "for" part will naturally flow from our lives without any real self-effort on our part.

And thus, I now understand why it's called the Great Amen. Because for every other time we say Amen ("I believe this to be true"), if we understand what it is we are saying "Amen" to in this prayer, suddenly we become Mary. We are sitting at His feet, loving Him and allowing Him to love us. We start having a real relationship with Him—instead of being like Martha and trying through our own efforts to do for Him and earn our way into His good graces.

Funny how many times I heard and said that prayer without even realizing there is no "for" in it. Through Him, with Him, in Him… and everything else will take care of itself. (2005)

Abide in Me

"If you abide in Me, and My words abide in you, ask whatever you wish, and it shall be done for you." --John 15: 7

Abide in me. Jesus invited his disciples to place their faith in His love as they walked to the Garden of Gethsemane that last fateful night. But He wasn't just talking to the disciples. He was talking to us, too. However, Jesus is not saying He wants us to walk *with* him. He is saying He wants us to remain *in* Him—as close as we could ever get to Him without being Him.

It wasn't until recently that I put words to this phenomenon. I knew it was in my life, but explaining it wasn't easy to do. At the time I called it "faith." As a writer, I put great faith in the belief that God would light my path, that if I surrendered the project to His care, I would have the right words at the right time.

The opportunities to use this faith were endless. For example, when my two year old deleted five pages of the new manuscript I was working on, I distinctly remember saying, "Well, I guess God didn't want it said that way." Or when my publicist said the cover for my second book (which I had chosen) would never work. It took me awhile before I surrendered and realized it was God that had a different idea. Sure enough when the new cover came into focus, it was far better than the original.

For several years these were the types of ways I tried to "abide in Him" although "faith" was probably the better term because I was still relying on some outside entity—not a spirit that permeated me.

Recently, however, I came into contact with Bruce Wilkinson's "Secrets of the Vine." After reading this book, I realized what had been happening for years. I believe this experience is the best definition for "abiding in me" around.

While writing my latest book, I received a magazine which gave me the very insight I needed to understand why a character was acting the way he was. Of course, everyone receives magazines every day, and it was one that I was subscribed to, so that shouldn't be all that noteworthy. Except for this: the post office had changed our address and that particular magazine was one I hadn't changed the address on yet. I hadn't received that magazine for more than four weeks, and when that copy got here, it was sent to the old address—an address which the post office had flatly refused to deliver to anymore. More than that, I haven't received any of the next three editions although I have now changed the address. So, why then did that one come through with exactly what I needed despite every obstacle against it?

I think the answer can be found in those three words: abide in me. Do we really think that some little post office crisis can keep God's plan from working in our lives? If so, then I challenge you to question how many of these "coincidences" in your life you are either missing out on—or overlooking right at this very moment.

As a firm believer in these words, I can tell you that if you will take them to heart... If you will accept that Jesus is not just an "out there entity" that you can have faith in but truly a spirit that permeates your very life... If you will truly accept His presence in every aspect of your life, every minute of every day, then He will abide in you, and your life will never again be the same.

After all it was His promise. (2002)

Thoughts on the Road to Emmaus

". . . their eyes were opened, and they recognized him . . ." – Luke 24:31

Two friends—people who had known Jesus, who had walked with Him, talked with Him, and eaten meals with Him every day for three years didn't recognize Him even on a long walk down a dusty road. Have you ever wondered about that? I have. How could that possibly be?

The reality is: the disciples were looking at a man who happened to be traveling along the same road they were. They did not see Jesus because they did not expect to see Jesus.

How many times on our walks through life do we not see Jesus? How many times do we talk with a co-worker or a parent or a child or a friend or even someone we have never met before and fail to recognize that this person holds a precious piece of Our Lord and Savior within them? And because we don't recognize Jesus in them, we treat them not as we would treat Jesus, but as just our friend, or just our co-worker, or just our child.

It must make Jesus terribly sad that for all our flowery words and pious presumptions, we still do not recognize Him in each other.

Moreover, consider this: Is it possible that in religious settings, we look at one another, and instead of seeing Jesus, we see only the other person's religion, their label? And because we don't see Jesus, we say, "You are so obviously not spiritual—look, you stand when we are kneeling, or you use crucifixes instead of picturing the risen Lord, or you pray to statues and icons instead of to the living God, or you don't have our label, and so, obviously God is not going to let you into His kingdom."

Thus, we spend so much time questioning each other's commitment to Jesus and so much time fighting over man-made rules and laws that we forget about those people who are lost and hurting. We forget to do God's real work—ministering to those who are hungry for His word and His truths to come into their lives. Instead, having been seduced by Satan to believe that God's kingdom is some kind of exclusive club, we spend our time fighting with each other about who is going to get in and completely fail to see that the world is going to hell around us.

However, we have the choice to open our eyes and commit ourselves to do God's work here on earth. Rather than judging, we can reach out to the lost souls—not by telling them about God's love, but by showing them how great God's love is. Witnessing by how we live and how we treat one another, so that they look to us and say, "I want to be like them. I want what they have." And then maybe God's grace will touch their hearts and make them ask, "How do I get it? What do they have that I don't?"

But living this way hinges on whether or not we see Jesus in every single person we happen to walk down a path with in our day-to-day lives. When we look at another person, do we see someone who is worthy of Christ's message? Someone whom God loves beyond measure? Do we see Jesus Himself—lost, hurting, and alone? Or do we see just another person.

I tell you truly, whatever you did not do for one of the least of these, you did not do for me. —Matthew 25:45

Think about the inherent admonition in these words. Our goal should be to treat others not as we want to be treated but as we would treat Jesus Himself. That is God's real work. We are commissioned to spend our time ministering to God's children—rather than trying to improve our status in His eyes or to impress one another.

By opening our eyes to Jesus' presence in those around us, we will come to see His spirit manifesting in our own lives. And thus we can say as the disciples did at the conclusion to the Emmaus story,

"Were not our hearts burning within us while He was speaking to us on the road." —Luke 24:32

Open your eyes. This opportunity is with you right now. Don't waste this chance to get to know the Jesus who is in your midst at this very moment. (2001)

A Second Look at Emmaus

For years the story of the walk to Emmaus fascinated me. In fact, it was one of the first topics I wrote about when I started doing articles. What is really cool though is when in one weekend, Jesus can take a story that you've heard a half a million times and shine the light on it differently so that it looks totally new. Like a diamond reflecting light from a different cut-angle it will take your breath away with how beautiful it is and more so with the intriguing depth that can hide in one little nugget of truth.

That was what happened to me this weekend with the story of Emmaus. The awesome thing to me is how many different perspectives God gave me so that I could see more hidden insights held in that story than I ever had in the past. It started the night before I even went to church. My friend who is teaching Sunday school called and asked if I had any insights to give her on what she might use to teach the road to Emmaus story the next morning.

Of course, I led with the thoughts recounted in my previous article about what it meant that the friends of Jesus didn't recognize him as they walked. I said that's often how we are in that we don't recognize Jesus in those who are walking this journey of life with us. We think of them as "only" our friend or our spouse or our child. Too often, we fail to recognize Jesus in them.

As we talked, I offered a few more thoughts, and then we hung up. The next morning my family traveled to the town where my sister lives for her oldest boy's First Communion. The priest giving the homily took a different look at it. He said that to understand the story, you had to know that Emmaus was a seat of Roman power at the time. The Biblical significance of that is that these two disciples were walking away from Jerusalem and Jesus and toward the Roman power. It wasn't until Jesus went and got them, showed them who he was and that he was alive, that they turned back and went back to Jerusalem.

Interesting. I'd never heard the story from that perspective.

Later that day, talking with my dad about the sermon they had heard at their church on the same reading, he gave me a slightly different take on it. He said that their priest had said the disciples were not walking away to Emmaus, as in having a casual stroll for no good reason. No. They were escaping. They were running (or walking really fast) from all that had happened in Jerusalem.

Then, as I put them all together, I saw what God so often does when we really take the time to look. I saw the layers of parallel meaning form so that what was happening in the physical realm, paralleled the mental and emotional, which paralleled the spiritual.

Here were these two disciples. They were walking away. They had turned their backs—literally—on Jerusalem and thus on Jesus and the whole idea of Christianity. They had seen what happened to Christ, and they physically wanted no part of that, so they were getting the heck out of Dodge so to speak. In the spirit realm, they had decided that Christianity wasn't worth it, so they were going to head toward what in worldly terms looked safe—the Roman command post. They were not only walking away from Christianity. They were walking toward the empty promises of the world.

And then, Jesus showed up. But they didn't see Him being Jesus—just as we often don't see Him when He shows up after we have strayed. He's come to invite us to come back, but we are so caught up in ourselves that we fail to recognize Him. Sure, we hear the song that touches our heart and calls us back. Yet we don't recognize that song as being Jesus walking with us even in our hurt and fear. Instead we keep walking, thinking that something in the world is going to fix what's wrong in our lives. Still, He walks with us, stride for stride, until maybe we've gone the whole seven miles into the heart of the world.

At that point it seems that He plans to continue on with His journey because He is not going to stay where He isn't wanted. But then for whatever reason we say, "No. Stop here. Stay the evening with us." And so He does—willingly, gladly. In fact, that's what He was hoping we would say all along. We sit down with Him at supper, and it isn't until He takes the bread and breaks Himself again for us that we recognize Who it is that has been with us all along.

At that moment we jump for joy, our hearts leap inside us because we realize that where we are—in the hurt and the fear of the world—is not where we have to stay. No, we have the option to go back to Jerusalem, to be with Jesus each and every moment. Of course that was always an option. It's just that sometimes that option looks so tough that walking into the world begins to look like an easier choice.

Rest assured, not a mile down that road, Jesus will show up. He will walk with you and talk with you, and then, He will gently invite you back. Wow. How cool is that?

Just makes me wonder what Jesus has in store for me on the third look at the Emmaus story sometime in the future. I know I will forever be grateful for this second look. It taught me so much about the extent of His love for each of us. It's so awesome that He is willing to walk that road to Emmaus every time circumstances make us think that going in the direction of the world looks like a good idea. I, for one, will now remember that going to Emmaus solves nothing. It's Jerusalem where I want to be. How about you? (2005)

As

"Forgive us our trespasses as we forgive those who trespass against us."
-- *The Our Father*

The most perfect prayer. The one Jesus told us, "When you pray, pray like this." Ever since, we've been praying the words He taught us. In fact, we've prayed it so often that many of us don't even think about what we're saying anymore. We run through the words almost unconsciously – memorized to the point that we no longer have to concentrate on what we're saying to say it.

But let me tell you, saying this line without really thinking about what it means is a scary proposition. Why? Because you are asking for exactly the same treatment you've been dishing out. So the question becomes – what have you been dishing out?

Are you judgmental? Do you judge situations and people without really getting to know them? Do you practice quiet prejudice – boxing people in and labeling them because of some outward characteristic? Then when you say "as," you've just asked God to judge you on the same scale. Are you petty? Do you watch for the faults of others and then make sure to point those out to everyone within earshot? Then you've given God permission to pick out and point out each and every one of your faults. Are you jealous? Do you judge actions without bothering to learn the whole story? Are you exacting? Harsh? Impossible to please? Do you brush by people because they have the wrong kind of jeans or the wrong accent or the wrong personality?

Think about what you're setting up for yourself. By saying "as," think about what you've told God to do when you stand before the Throne.

The good news is that "as" works just as thoroughly in a positive direction. Do you have mercy on those around you? Do you forgive? Put the past behind you and truly move on? Do you bless those who have hurt you and pray for those who hate you? Do you actively look for the good even when it seems buried?

If so, that is the scale God will use for you. It's a smart thing to remember the next time you blithely say "as I forgive those…" (2003)

My Timing is Perfect

"Make me know Thy ways, O Lord; Teach me Thy paths."
--Psalm 25:4

There are days when I get really frustrated with man's place in religion. It probably has to do with how and where I was brought up. In a little town with only one church and one faith practiced, I didn't often see the edge of the power of change that the hierarchy of a religious community can wield. Church was the same; believers were the same; God was the same no matter where I went. That's probably why all the changes the Church is making now upset me so much. Growing up, my religion was as solid as my faith. Now, however, I realize that the ideal I had always believed in back then simply does not exist.

No, in this world people want excitement and challenge. One way to stir excitement is by making changes. Make a change, and suddenly everyone is compelled to take a stand on the issue—for or against. The hierarchy then gains power by holding fast to the change they have decreed. Eventually the multitudes surrender to the change, which confirms who has the power. Until, of course, someone new comes along and needs to make a change to reassert power, and the whole process repeats itself.

In the last few years, my religion has gone through many changes. We've been told that instead of kneeling at one part of the Mass, we are now to stand (then we went back to kneeling). We've been told that instead of only receiving Communion on the tongue it is now acceptable even encouraged to receive by hand. We've been told that children should no longer be Confirmed at 15 when they are able to make their own choice, it is now better to have them make their Confirmations as 8-year-olds because Confirmation cannot be "learned or earned."

Of course my mind which had to study for a year to be able to pass the test on the religious teachings of the church in order to "earn" Confirmation wonders how we have suddenly gone so far in the other direction. This concern was intensified when my eight-year-old daughter arrived at this juncture of her life. I had hoped and prayed, literally, that the rules would be changed back—as some had said they might be. However, during our first meeting for second grade parents, we found out it was not to be. The second graders would be Confirmed as per the decree of the hierarchy.

For weeks I vacillated between fury and bewilderment. I didn't understand why the religion I had grown up with looked so different than the one I was passing on to my child. I argued with people, asking why this change was made, and what my options were in going forward. I couldn't figure out how I could ever be at peace with myself if I took the central decision of my life away from my child. But I also couldn't figure out how I would be at peace if it was God's will and I stood in the way of that.

Then one night after a meeting, my heart hurt so badly that I was near tears. I held my daughter's hand as she drifted off to sleep and looking at her, I finally begged God, "Please, I don't understand this. I know You know that I want what's best for her, and I know what's best for Her is Your will. Please help me to know what that is, and help me to be at peace with whatever happens."

Instantly a voice in my head said very patiently, "My timing is perfect for each child. She is Mine, give her to Me, and whatever happens will be what I had envisioned for her." With tears rolling down my face, I did just that. I let go of the control I had been gripping so tightly. For the first time, I had true peace about not just Confirmation but about her whole life.

She's God's child, and God will guide her life the way it is supposed to go. I'm God's child too, and God's timing, if I let it be, will always be perfect for me just as it will be for all of us—no matter what changes men make in the rules. (2003)

Smoke

I always thought Ecclesiastes was like Proverbs. That's probably because of the "to every time there is a season. . ." passage. So when a friend of mine read Ecclesiastes from *The Message,* I wasn't prepared for her reaction.

Her first comment was, "It makes no sense." I tried to get her to explain that. She couldn't. She just kept saying things like "It's so negative. He just keeps saying everything is smoke. It makes no sense." Finally in desperation, she said, "You read it, and see if it makes sense to you."

Now I know a nudge from the Holy Spirit when I see one. So I went the next day and started reading. She was right. It was negative. It didn't seem to fit in the Bible at all. Depressing is a word that comes to mind.

Throughout the whole book, the writer talks about life as smoke, an illusion. He says it's pointless because all you do is work and work and then you die. What is the point?

At first, I was as taken aback as my friend, but as I kept reading, I realized what he was really saying. Life lived by the world's standards of success and fulfillment IS smoke. It's an illusion, and the saddest thing in the whole world is to get to the end before you realize that.

I belong to several writing groups – Christian ones mainly. As January rolled around several groups talked about the individuals' goals for this year. I will never forget one post. It read simply:

"My only goal this year is to get this silly novel rewritten and published."

In light of what I now see through Ecclesiastes, this is a tragic statement. This person is focused totally on the smoke. She believes that once her novel is published, then life will really begin. She is not excited about the prospects of learning from the rewrites or even the connections with other people she may make in the publishing process. In short when and if she publishes her "silly novel," I'm quite sure she will be left asking the Anthony Robbins' question: "Is this all there is?"

At that point she may think that when she gets *two* books published, THEN life will really start happening. It's such a lie. It's such a trap. And yet, it's a trap many, many people are living in today.

My friend asked, "How do you make sure you're not just going for the smoke?" To which I said, "Make the right things important, and the right 'things' aren't things – they are people."

So often in our headlong rush to get the smoke, we fail to take notice of those weary travelers on life's road with us who need our help—emotional, spiritual, and/or physical. We have the means and the opportunity to help them, yet we are so focused on getting the smoke that we pass up that chance completely.

Because of the lesson of Ecclesiastes, I now know that when I get to Heaven, my awards and accomplishments will amount to water through a sieve. The only thing that will be real is the love I have extended and to how many people I have extended it. Everything else is just smoke. (2005)

Risk In the Real World

*And when He had finished speaking, He said to Simon, "Put out
into the deep water and let down your nets for a catch." And
Simon Peter answered, "Master, we worked hard all night and
caught nothing, but at Your bidding I will let down the nets."
And when they had done this, they enclosed a great quantity of
fish; and their nets began to break... --Luke 5:4-7*

'Put out into the deep water.' How many of us never take
the time to really understand the significance of these words?
We are too busy floating along and trying to stay in control on
the shallow water to even think of putting out to the deep water.
But why did Jesus tell the apostles to put out to the deep water?

Simple. That's where the fish were. To understand why,
you must understand the principles and the assumptions that the
apostles were making. First, at this time, there were no motors.
When you were on the water, you were at the mercy of the wind
and the elements, and the further out you went, the more this
was true and the less the chance that you were going to make it
back to the shore. In fact, it was the fishermen who were the real
risk-takers in Jesus' time. These were men who finessed the
boundaries of safety just to do their jobs on an everyday basis.

So, when Jesus told Peter to put out into the deep water,
Peter knew well what the deep water represented—risk.

Ultimate risk. Death if the winds caught the boat and they couldn't get back to the shore. The very act of obeying the command shows Peter's faith. What he couldn't know was what the Lord already did. Every other fisherman in the region had already fished in the shallow water. It was out in the deep that the overwhelming quantities of fish could be found.

This lesson is no less true today and was recently brought into focus for me in a very modern-day way. As a webmaster, one of my tasks is to get people to know my site exists. In doing this, I have taken several avenues—one of which is having an on-going link campaign. In layman's terms, this means going out surfing for hours, searching for sites to approach to ask if they would be willing to link to my site, and thus give surfers one more way to find me. It is a time-consuming and very often frustrating undertaking.

Because I write Inspirational Romance, I try to contact sites that fit into one of the following categories: Christian, women, writing, and romance. Now, let's talk risk. On one side, I have people who are adamant about traditional values, family-friendly messages, and staunch, unbending Christianity. On the other side I have romance sites, which often bend toward decidedly un-Christian values. I find myself on the tightrope in between, wishing that both could understand how close they really are. In our society we have unfortunately gotten the message that romance and God are mutually exclusive. The reason of course is that romance is equated with sex outside of marriage, and God condemns these kinds of practices. The very fact that I choose to write Inspirational Romance should tell you that I don't buy into this myth. To me, there is nothing more holy than a man and woman who have committed themselves to each other through God's love.

For this cause a man shall leave his father and mother, and shall cleave to his wife; and the two shall become one flesh.
--Ephesians 5: 31

The problem is too many who equate romance with prurient sex base the opening days of a relationship on sex and believe that they have to because "everybody else does." Thus, no one puts God into the relationship until they are ready to get married. Then they want the big church wedding, and the soul-fulfilling notion of standing before God and man to commit themselves to each other—although they haven't bothered to acknowledge God's presence in the relationship until that moment. And we wonder why the divorce rate is high. Wouldn't it be far better to promote a message that encourages couples to invite God into the relationship from the very beginning, trusting in Him to guide both partners, and believing that if it is meant to work in His great plan, it will? This is the message that I'm trying to get out.

However, this is not a message that is even an option on many sites labeled "romance." Nonetheless, because I believe this is an option that no one should go into a relationship without being exposed to, I try to put my site link on pages that promote romance, which means they are listed on pages with the romance equals sex idea. This upsets some of the Christian sites that I approach. Now I'm not saying this message is on my site, it is in linking to sites that have this on their sites that I get into trouble.

Of course, my other option is to absolutely not allow any site with anything resembling this message linking with mine (knowing that my link won't be on their site because of this policy and thus will not be on many if any romance sites). Thus, when someone searches for romance, their options will be only those sites which relate to pleasure at its basest—with no mention of God or how truly beautiful real romance with God in the center can be. Maybe it's me, but I think this is sad.

And so, I am left with the choice of preaching only to the choir or going out in the deep, knowing the risks I'm taking but feeling that Christ is in fact in my boat and will get me safely back to shore. It's a risk I'm willing to take for all those poor souls out there who see no connection between God and romance. To me, that would be a terrible place to live. (2002)

Miracles Happen

I know miracles happen because I've witnessed one first hand. I'd like to take the credit for it, but the truth is all I did was step out on a limb that I was sure might snap at any moment. The limb was called sending a little unsolicited help to someone in dire need of some. At the time the person I sent it to was going through a messy, heart-wrenching divorce only a year after saying vows he thought would carry him through a lifetime. The young lady whom we all thought the world of turned out to have more secrets than most of us accumulate in a lifetime. They tried to make it work, but when a beautiful piece of fruit is rotten to the core, saving it in its present form is pointless.

Devastated and alone, this young man whom I have always greatly admired for his forthrightness, determination, and heart suddenly lost the sparkle in his eyes. He looked so sad—like he had given up on life itself. I prayed and sent good thoughts his way, but still his eyes haunted me. Then a book came into my possession. Upon reading it, I thought that if anything could make a difference, maybe this had a shot. I knew he would think I was insane for sending it—the way we all think that others are appalled when we go outside without make-up when in reality they are too busy worrying about their own bad hair day to notice. So, I took a deep breath, put his address on it, and sent it, figuring that would be the last I would hear about it.

A month or so later, this young man's sister, who is a closer friend to me than he is, asked what book I gave him. I told her the title and asked, "Why?" She said he had read the whole thing even though he isn't a reader and had then gone and bought four copies to give to friends. She was wondering because she wanted to get a copy for herself. I was in a little shock, but I was happy he had made good use of it.

But never could I have prepared myself for what happened next. Apparently he gave a copy to his parents who began raving about the book to anyone who would listen. His sister and her husband finished it and had a similar reaction. By this point my mom was busting with curiosity to read it so she asked the sister if she could borrow her copy. When the sister brought the copy to my mom, MY sister happened to be there. Now my sister had heard all the wonderful stories about the book... How the original young man had found new faith in God from it, how his parents had embraced a new day and let go of the hurt and anger at the situation, how even the people that the young man worked with had started to turn around because of it.

Before my mom could get the copy, however, my little sister grabbed it and said she had been wanting to read it. Now, I knew that my little sister had gone through severe depression years ago, but I had honestly thought she had moved past it and on to a life that she was enjoying.

A few days after this musical book exchange (which I didn't even know about until later), my little sister called me with awe in her voice, "Do you know what you did?" I wasn't exactly sure what she meant. Then she went on to tell me how she had gotten to a point in her life that she believed life on earth was just a living hell and that she might as well find a way to survive it because she certainly wasn't enjoying it. She was berating her kids, quarreling with everybody, mad at the world, and hurt besides. In short she had given up on ever finding God or happiness.

Then she started hearing about this book and how it was helping everyone else. After reading it, she told me, "This is what everyone who is in pain needs to hear. They need to understand this. It makes all the difference in the world."

At this writing she is still battling physical pain that she has had for years; however, I sincerely hope that by stepping out on that limb of faith, I have helped her find an emotional peace that I don't think she has ever had. The most amazing thing is that had it not been for the tragedy of the first young man, I never would have thought to give the book to my sister. For going out on that limb of faith, God rescued lives I never even knew were in jeopardy.

By now, I'm sure you're wondering about the title of this truly incredible book. Its name is *The Greatest Miracle in the World*. It's by Og Mandino. It's very short, very easy to read, and very, very powerful. If you know someone who needs a miracle in their lives, run—don't walk—to your nearest bookstore. Send it to them, give it to them, read it for yourself.

According to my sister, you need do no more than simply present the opportunity. Don't say, "You need to read this." Just say, "I read this and enjoyed it, and I thought you might to."

What miracles does God have lined up when you read this message? I have no idea, but I took one leap of faith to send it to someone the first time and saw infinitesimal results that I'm still in awe over. So basically, I'm not limiting anything God decides to do with this book and a little prompting from me anymore. Why? Because I'm here to attest: Miracles happen. (2004)

You Can Come To Me

The sitcom set-up was easy enough. In fact, I could follow it while carrying on an in depth conversation with a friend of mine about the amazing love of the Holy Spirit. The set-up amounted to this: The father, a widower, was being pressured into "getting on with his life." Realizing that he was hanging on, he decided his friends were right, and he took off his wedding ring, determined to go on the date he'd been set up on. As he was on the date, however, his two young daughters, upset by the thought of their father dating again, got into a fight and inadvertently knocked the wedding ring down the sink.

In true sitcom fashion the situation quickly deteriorated all the way to the two girls trying to take the sink apart to get the ring out. Of course, by the time anyone found them, the bathroom was flooded and there was a huge mess. At about that time, my conversation with my friend wound to a close, and we stood to go into the television room. The show had come to the high point. The father sat down with the oldest girl, and he said, "You know you can come to me with anything."

With her head down, the young girl says sadly, "I know I should've come to you right away, but I panicked."

Isn't that exactly what God says to each of us? He wants us to come to Him in our most difficult times. In fact, He wants us to come *before* we've flooded the bathroom and made a real mess of things. He wants us to trust His love enough to be able to come to Him and let Him help us. However, too often, we are like the young daughter, "I know I should've come to you right away, but I panicked."

Don't panic. He loves you, and He wants to help. Go to Him. Tell Him what happened. He won't get mad. He won't throw you out of His house on your ear. No. He won't. Remember the parable of the Prodigal Son? He will be so glad you turned around and came back, He won't even let you get through your carefully prepared speech about what you should've done, could've done, would've done... He loves you so much He'll throw His arms around you and throw a party!

In Him, you've got an ally like no other. Don't panic. He's on your side. He wants to help. The only question is, will you let Him before you've made a total mess of things? It's your choice. (2004)

The Crystal Ball

Wouldn't it be nice to be able to see into the future? Especially at those times in life when the road forks, and you have no idea which fork is the best choice. You could choose X, and it could work out marvelously—or it could be a total flop. Or you could not choose X and wish for the rest of your life you had.

Recently I've found just such a crystal ball. No, it doesn't literally allow us to see into the future, but it does allow for the best decision to be made at every fork in the road every single time. What is this crystal ball? Where can you get one?

Well, think for a moment. If I had this crystal ball, what would you be willing to pay for it? Would it be worth ten dollars? A hundred? A thousand? Remember, it will unerringly tell you exactly what is the best thing to do every single time. Surely that would be worth a few dollars in a trade.

Now, what would you say if I told you that this crystal ball is monetarily free. That's right. It costs nothing at all... However, it does require something, and that something is giving up the control you think you have over a situation. It means giving up the notion that you know what the best outcome in a situation is. Here is reality: You don't. You can't. You don't have all of the information to *know* what is the best outcome in a situation.

But if you don't, then who does? One name: God.

Of course, God who is everywhere in all times and all moments knows. Why? Because unlike you, he can see the whole picture. He can see every ramification of every possible decision in any given situation that you can make. In short, He can see with perfect clarity the choice you should make.

While listening to Bruce Wilkinson's excellent audio, "A Life God Rewards," I heard one line that he really doesn't go on to discuss and expand on. It's more of a transition line pulling together two other thoughts. However, in that line, I realized a lesson that I had used but hadn't put words to. He said:

"As the only person to come from eternity to earth and then return to eternity, Jesus knows the whole truth—past, present, and future—and can give you a one of a kind perspective," Wilkinson says. "For example, he can see your present from a moment far out in your infinite future and tell you exactly how to prepare for what is to come."

Wow! What an unbelievable crystal ball that is! Think about it. If Jesus loves you beyond measure and He wants only what is best for you in the long run (and that means the really long run of eternity), doesn't it make sense to allow Him to guide your life right now?

Unfortunately that's not how most of us pray. We say things like, "God, if you'll only let me get this job, then I'll be happy." "God, I just need a way to get to work. I'll be perfectly happy with that 20-year-old Honda. Please, if I can just have that…" And God says, "Well, okay, I really wanted to give you this brand new Lexus, but I want to make you happy, so here's your Honda."

What I'm suggesting here is a radical change in thinking. Instead of being outcome-specific in our prayers, wouldn't it be better to take our hands off the wheel and let Jesus decide what's best for us?

True story, my first book had been in the hands of one company for more than a year. They had been promising during the course of that year that it would be out "next month." However, the "next months" had strung together to make a year, and I was getting frustrated. Throughout the course of the year,

I had gotten these little pushes that I was to put out a second book with a different company, but I resisted. I didn't want two books out at the same time. I didn't want anyone in the first company mad because I went with a second company. In short, I was paralyzed by a decision that could radically change my future, and I wasn't at all sure which choice to make.

So, I made a deal with God. I basically told Him that I didn't know what He wanted me to do, and I didn't want to make a mistake. So if He didn't want me to put out the second book, He needed to get someone from company one to contact me in the next two weeks. Then I put that decision aside and went to work on other things. When the deadline came, I still hadn't heard anything, so I said, "Okay, 24 more hours, and then I send it in."

Still nothing. So I sent the second book. Two days later company one emailed to give me a publicist. When she later questioned the second book, I said, "God made the decision not me." You know, I have never regretted that decision—even though it was highly unconventional.

I'm not saying you should go around giving God ultimatums. I now realize a simpler method is just to put every day in His hands. Give Him the reins of deciding what's most important for your time. Then when things work out, you know it was His will. When things don't work out like you expected, it was His will, and He has a better idea.

Then all you have to do is do your best, work as hard as you can, and let Him make the decisions. Pray only for guidance and for peace no matter what happens, and I think you will be amazed at the number of incredible answers that will start popping up in your life. (2003)

The Rules

There are at least two versions of the Ten Commandments. Did you know that? There is a Protestant version and a Catholic version. I didn't know that until about two years ago while watching a video for kids on the Ten Commandments, I suddenly noticed their numbers were off. Five was suddenly something I didn't recognize. Oh, no wait. I did recognize it, but it wasn't five. Of course, I thought they'd made a mistake. I mean it took me a long time to memorize those commandments in order, so if I was right, then they had to be wrong. Right?

It now amazes me how focused on the rules we as Christians are. We learn them, teach them, memorize them, and then proceed to use them to bop each other over the head with them.

While shopping at a Christian bookstore this afternoon, my ears suddenly caught on an angry voice at the main counter. As I listened, it became very clear this gentleman had found something wrong in the store because he was *demanding* that they take the offending item off the shelf. The manager calmly explained that first he didn't have the power to do that and secondly that the item was based on a certain version of the Bible.

Now, I'll admit I'm not a Biblical scholar. I know the Catholic version adds books toward the beginning, but other than that, if I simply picked a version off the shelf, I couldn't tell you what version it was. So, the two men proceeded over to the Bible shelves, which happened to be right next to where I was shopping.

Having gone through this fruitless exercise myself, I knew what they would find. There are no numbers to the commandments as listed in the Bible. Sure enough, the man said, "Well, all the words are there, but they combined this first one and then chopped the last one into two. That's not right. I want to talk to the store owner."

The manager had no choice. He got the store owner. In minutes they were back. The store owner said that the salesman she had purchased the posters from had explained that the poster he now held was the Catholic version of the Commandments. Well, that was just ridiculous. The Commandments are the Commandments. They don't change. Do they?

I seriously considered stepping in but decided against it. I'm sure you're asking, "Why? You should step in and defend your faith." Ah, but I wouldn't have been defending my *faith*. I would've been defending my *religion*. And the difference is gaping.

You see, my faith is that I believe God is right in my heart every minute of every day. My faith says His Spirit guides my every step. My faith says He loves me no matter what, and I am only to follow His voice and let Him lead. My *religion* says the Commandments are supposed to be numbered a certain way. My *religion* says this is the code you must follow to be considered a member of this religion.

There was a time when my religion was more important to me than my faith because I really didn't understand the difference. Now I do. So, to me, it really doesn't matter what order we put the rules in. What matters is how we are living our lives every moment of every day. The very real question you have to ponder is this: Is my faith about the order of the rules or is it about God? Once we get that in order, we can stop arguing about what Number Five is because it won't matter anymore anyway. But it is interesting how indignant we become when somebody goes changing the rules we've learned on us. I mean, goodness, when you're living by the rules, it's hard enough to get it right even when they don't change! (2005)

What Everyone Else Says

Talk about confused, my friend was. She kept saying, "I just cry and say, 'Lord, please tell me what's the truth.'" Understanding her plight wasn't difficult. She was learning something new and needing for it to be right the first time. So she did what any sane person would do, she asked for help. Only the "help" sounded like this:

"You have to have a lot of details."

"You use too many details."

"I like this section."

(Same section) "This section needs a lot of work."

"I like this character."

(Same character) "I hate this character."

"You need a hook."

"Hooks are for the book, not the cover letter."

"You have to do this." "Don't ever do this."

In short, she was drowning in the sea of conflicting advice.

As we talked, she began to see the conflicting advice for what it was – other people's opinions. As my mom always said, "Give me your opinion. I want to hear it, but I don't have to take it."

My friend was heading the opinions and trying to use all of them, and it was paralyzing her. It's a trap many of us fall into. Everyone has an opinion about how we should be living our lives. We should do this. We have to do this. We can't do that. And many times we get completely conflicting advice. We, too, can be drowning and wondering if there even is a "truth."

After about 15 minutes of hearing about how she didn't understand because all of these advice-givers were multi-published authors, and they should know the truth, in frustration I finally said, "Yes, but they are not God." That stopped her cold.

The truth is that there is no problem with asking for advice, but then you must make the decision for yourself. Some will agree with you. Some will not. But trying to please everybody will soon convince you that nothing you do is right. It will paralyze you, and that's exactly what Satan would love to do.

I suggested that she get quiet, breathe, and listen to what her heart was telling her to do. In all likelihood it won't look like what the world says is "the only thing that will work" because God doesn't work the way the world does. In fact, His direction may sound absolutely crazy (Christ on the cross comes to mind). However, if you don't have Him guiding you, finding "the truth" is all-but impossible.

Five minutes after I got off the phone from our conversation, I got in my van to get my kids from school. Sean Hannity happened to be on the radio talking to a soldier who had been ridiculed by an anti-war protester.

Hannity said, (I paraphrase), "You can't live your life based on what everyone else things – especially if you are to take a real stand. If you make everyone else happy, you will be paralyzed because whatever you do will always be wrong. You have to figure out where you are and be there." After at least a three-minute speech, he took a breath and said, "Whew, I don't know where that came from. Why did I go into that?"

I laughed. It was a message to me verifying what I had just said sent from the Holy Spirit through Sean Hannity over the airwaves even though Sean had no idea that's why he said it. It's pretty cool how the Holy Spirit can get that stuff to work out. (2004)

The Light

Your word is a lamp to my feet and a light for my path. Psalm
119:104

My dad always says that God doesn't put the light on
your head so you can see way out into the future, He puts it at
your feet so you can see the next step. While doing a walk
recounting Jesus' journey to Calvary, I was with a large group of
women. The walk began at dusk and continued as the light
around us faded and slowly vanished.

The leaders had given each of us a battery-operated
candle. A single light. I hadn't used mine most of the trip—
preferring to walk the pseudo-journey up the Via Dolorosa in the
dimming light as the world shut itself off around me.

Then as we rounded the curve after Jesus was crucified
and on the way to see Him laid in the tomb, I realized that the
older lady next to me was holding her candle closer to the
walkway in an apparent attempt to see so she would not stumble.
Immediately I took my candle out of my pocket and turned it on
to help.

Unfortunately those candles were made to inspire the
soul—not to light darkened walkways. My mind immediately
said, "Gee, Stace, fat lotta good your puny little candle did." At
that moment from directly behind me, someone turned on a
mega-watt flashlight, and the whole walk was clearly visible.

In that instant, I got it. I don't have to light the whole way for those around me. All I have to do is turn my candle on, and Jesus' light will be right there to back me up. I simply must have the courage to believe in His light rather than relying on my own so that I never think that I have to do it all myself. It was a lesson I needed to hear, and one I'm eternally glad He sent me on a walk through the gift He gave me. (2004)

Both

Blessings. We talk about them, pray about them, give thanks for them, and sometimes we even feel very guilty about getting them. Although the Bible says God is "able to do exceedingly abundantly beyond all that we ask or think, according to the power that works within us," we worry about and we question how serious He really was when He made that promise.

The cycle goes something like this. We hit rock bottom and remember God might be able to help, so we start praying. We ask, and as He promised, things start looking up. We keep praying because by now it has become a habit. Slowly then more quickly more blessings show up—some that we prayed for, some we never saw coming. Then the guilt slides through us. "Look at all He's given me. How could I even think of asking for more? I mean, isn't that greedy?" So we quit asking until we're in trouble again.

In truth, the paradox is we can never ask God for too much. Why? Because God is limitless, boundless, infinite. There is literally no limit to God's love or to His desire to pour that love into and through our lives onto others. Satan knows this, so he uses our best instincts against us. "Don't be greedy. You have enough. Don't ask for more." "Think about those who don't have as much as you have. Take your fair share, and be satisfied with that." "Aren't you ashamed of yourself for even asking God about something like that? He doesn't have time to listen to such petty concerns." And on and on.

Unfortunately, he's good at it. He has us convinced that there are things too small for God to worry about in our lives. He has us convinced that if things are good, asking for more is asking too much of God. Worst of all, he has us convinced that God has set some sort of invisible limit on what He will give us, and if we cross that line, God will be so angry He will take all the blessings we now have away.

Lies. It's all lies, and yet we buy into it, and we live our lives afraid to ask for the blessings God wants to give us.

Take my friend for example. She was recently lamenting because God in His goodness had provided the perfect apartment for her (after she specifically asked for it). Then He provided the perfect car for her (after she asked for it). Then she stumbled into asking for the thing she most wants—a God-centered man who would come into her life and love her the way she is now loving everyone else. That seemed just too much to ask for, especially after she'd already gotten the other blessings.

She said, "I just feel so greedy wanting it all." As if the Holy Spirit opened a lesson book, she went on, "It's like the other day. I was at the store, and there was this little girl in front of me in line. She walked up with two pieces of candy. The cashier rang it up and said, 'That'll be $1.93.' Unfortunately all this little girl had was $1.

"The cashier said, 'Look. You've got two pieces of candy, but you don't have enough money to buy both, so you're going to have to put one of them back. Which one do you want, and which one will you put back?'"

My friend said, "She was a little girl, and it was candy. Of course she wanted both of them!" The situation became more tense as the cashier began demanding that the little girl make a choice. Then my friend reached into her own purse, pulled out a dollar, slid it to the cashier, and said, "Let her have both of them." She said, "I was just so grateful for all the blessings He's given me, I wanted to share those blessings with someone else."

At the end of her story, I said, "You know what He's trying to tell you through that, right?" She just looked at me as if she hadn't realized there was a message. So, I continued.

Look at it this way: You are the little girl. You want both things. Satan is the cashier, looking at you with a sneer saying, "No. You don't have enough to pay for both. You can only have one, so which one will it be? Make a choice already. I've got other people waiting."

And then God who is standing at your side the whole time, without being asked, slips the full payment to Satan and says, "Let her have both of them. It's on Me."

The truth is, He wants to do that for you. The only stipulation is you must be open to receiving His blessings in your life. By now, He and I have a standing agreement. I'm open. Whatever He wants to send my way is fine by me. In fact, I often simply pray, "All Your best in my life today, God."

Over and over, He has sent blessings I never even saw coming. Friends to support me in times of need, others who He could love through me, moments of such awe-inspiring closeness with Him I have either laughed out loud or cried. I call that exceedingly abundant beyond all that we could ask or think. Wouldn't you? (2005)

2

On You

For I know the plans I have for you, declares the Lord plans to prosper you and not to harm you, plans to give you hope and a future.   -Jeremiah 29:11

You Are God's Master Piece

A Piece for your pocket
To remember today
That God placed you here
to walk along His way.

Your purpose is sure,
Your path is straight.
Your future is set
But it isn't fate.

God's love is with you.
God's love is true.
He loved you first
Even before you were you.

So remember you weren't
Random; You were made
With a plan; to fit into His work
As only you can!

Practice

Very few of us can pick up a complex task and ace it the first time we try it. Take typing. In all the years I taught it, I never had a single student sit down at the keyboard and type 60-70 words a minute their first time.

Not long ago a writing friend of mine asked me to explain how I learned to write. I told her, "I wrote." To which she replied, "Well, yeah, but I mean how did you LEARN to write." Again I said, "I wrote." Journals, poems, short stories, articles, news stories, feature stories, songs, novels, essays. If it involved putting words together on paper, I did it.

It sounds simple but terribly time consuming. Wouldn't it be so much easier if there was just a formula you could give someone? Anyone new at anything wants to be able to do it like a pro the first time out. We all want to be able to play the guitar like Keith Urban or play basketball like Lebron James. But the reality is that even Keith Urban didn't play that way the first time he picked up a guitar. Same with Mr. James. Sure, they had some innate talent, but what they had more than that was enough desire to do it well, that they were willing to do what is in everybody's grasp—practice.

The first time I learned this rule, I was in fifth grade. The girls in my hometown were famous statewide because they made it to and won State Championships regularly in basketball. So, we all got to learn basketball whether we wanted to or not. Now, fortunately I was from a very small school, so our coach in the fifth grade was the same coach who steered the high school teams to these State Championships. I will forever be grateful for what I learned from him. In short, I learned the value of practice.

We didn't start by shooting at the goal. No, we started by learning where to put our hands on the basketball and where to put our feet on the floor. We "shot" with no ball at least a few hundred times at the beginning of each practice session. Then we practiced shooting an actual basketball into the air. Then we shot to each other. And when I say practice, I mean just that. Thousands of times set your hands, set your feet, down, up, follow through the air—to your partner who then went through the same procedure.

In the high school ranks, the girls on the team were required to make 2,000 free throws before the season began. At the time it seemed excessive. Now I understand. When you stand on that line and make 2,000 free throws and then make countless more during practices, by the time you step on that line with a gym-full of people yelling at you and the game on the line, your body knows what to do automatically.

Ask any good pianist, typist, cook, designer, soccer player... Ask anyone who is at the top of any game how they got there, and you will hear one refrain over and over even if it only echoes in their statements: They practiced. They came before everyone else, they concentrated on learning to do each step not just right but perfect while the actual practice was going, and they stayed after regular practice to work more. Top students spend hours reading and studying. Their success is no mystery. They practiced.

And the lesson transfers so easily to every area of our lives. Want to be more patient? Practice patience in the small situations so you'll be ready in the big situations. Want to be a better friend? Practice it. Want your kids to say "Please" and "Thank you"? Then they must practice it.

That's the key. It may take 2,000 times, but if the desire is there, proficiency will follow. I can't play basketball to save my life (too afraid of the other nine players on the court), but I can shoot the most beautiful set-shot and the most beautiful jump shot you've ever seen. Why?

Because I practiced. (2005)

You Already Have

About a year ago my goals changed radically. The first goal that changed was the one that said my ultimate goal was to get to Heaven and have God say, "Well done good and faithful servant." What I realized was, that goal was about me—what I would get, about what I thought I had earned, and about having Him be proud of me. When the understanding that it wasn't about me but about Him came through my life, I altered that goal to be this: What I want when I get to Heaven is for God to put His arms around me and say, "I love you." That's it. That's all I want. And you know what? He says that every day, so I know that goal is already met.

The second goal I had was about reaching people for God. I wanted to touch as many people as I could for Him. It sounded good, but again, that was about me—not about Him. It was about what I could do for Him. What a joke. The God who put the stars in the sky, formed everything from nothing, and designed it all to perfection, and I was going to do something for Him. Right. What I now understand is that He doesn't need me to do anything for Him, what He wants most is to live through me—just as He lived through Jesus.

Based on that understanding, in the last month or so I have altered my second goal as well. My "while I'm here" goal is now: I want anyone who looks at me to see Him—in my writing, in person, on the phone, however we happen to meet. The credit for everything that my life produces is His, not mine. For if He is living through me, it is Him who is doing whatever efforts happen to come through me, so He deserves the credit.

The cool thing about this is that this morning I was listening to a song I'd heard many times and really liked. The song is called "Song for Dad" by Keith Urban. It is one he never released. It's on his *Golden Road* album. It's about his dad and how as he gets older, he sees more things in his life that he realizes are things his dad did. Then toward the end of the song, there was a part that just blew me away. It says:

"Everything he ever did, he always did with love,
And I'm proud today to say I'm his son.
When somebody says, 'I hope I get to meet your dad,'
I just smile and say, 'You already have.'"

So now, that's my goal to be able to say that by meeting me they've already met my Father for He is living through me. That goal feels like a perfect fit in the way the others never did. The others put me in chains about what I had to do. These goals free me to simply live and watch what He does through me. It's an awesome way to live!   (2005)

Short Thoughts on Dreams

…Excerpt from "Dreams by Starlight" by Staci Stallings

'All that I can do is all that I must. For my dreams have been inscribed on my heart so deeply that they and me are now inseparable. As the stars are interwoven into the night sky, inextricably entwined, so my dreams are a part of me—no, they are me. I could no more set aside my dreams and walk away than a rose could set aside its scent and bloom without it. They and me are one.

'In the night before the light of my birth, my dreams were emblazoned into the fabric of that which would become my life. However, now, standing at the dawn of reaching for those dreams, unseen forces threaten to hurl them into the darkness of oblivion. For what? A few pennies? A few coins, which in the face of everything should mean nothing.

'Yet those few coins are beginning to mean everything to me. Everything. For like a gentle hand that at any moment could turn hostile and crush them before they are given their chance to shine, they hold the fragile porcelain of my dreams.

'In the absence of these precious pieces of metal, my dreams are as worthless as the dirt at my feet. Without them, the stars adorning the night sky could be nothing more than unattainable hallucinations in a mind that has held on too long to the belief that they are real and that they are reachable. If only..

'All that I can do is all that I must.'

(2000)

I'll Win It For You

The game was tight. Archrivals had faced off for three and a half periods in a seesaw battle that was going down to the wire. As the clock ticked down, the two sides traded the lead back and forth. Neither could be assured of victory because with the game so close, anything could happen.

From the sideline, the coach watched his team getting more and more apprehensive as the seconds ticked away. They were missing shots they never missed. They were missing opportunities they didn't miss. Even their body language said, "This is bad. We might lose this one."

With less than a minute left, the coach called a time out. Now he knew that every girl on that court had been over the plays a million times. They didn't need elaborate help to set up a play for a last second win. They needed to calm down and play the way they knew how to play. So when they bent into that huddle, the coach told them something more than a little unconventional. "Go out there. Play the game. Have fun. Do your best, and I'll win it for you."

No pressure instructions. No you have to win this or we lose to our rivals. No anxiety-inducing strategy. Simply, "Go play, and I'll win it for you."

To my way of thinking, that was an audacious statement because in reality, it wouldn't be the coach taking the shot that would win or lose the game. He would be standing on the sideline with no direct control whatsoever. However, this coach knew something about the training these girls had been through, and he knew without a doubt they could do it. The problem was *they* didn't know they could do it, and so, he let them rely not on themselves for the win but on him.

The amazing thing to me when I really started thinking about this statement is that what that coach told his team is exactly what Jesus tells each one of us: "Go out there. Play the game. Have fun. Do your best, and I'll win it for you."

We think it's all on us—that we have to get everything right, do everything perfectly, or our "win" will never materialize. In fact, we get sucked into this mentality that Heaven may be just out of our reach no matter what we do. However, I think the reality is that Jesus is the coach standing on the sideline having full faith that we can do everything He's trained us to do. We can love just like He's shown us. We can give; we can live—not because we can do it on our own but because He's right there, and He has faith that we have been given everything we need to win through Him.

I'm sure you know the end of the story. When the buzzer sounded, the team who had just gone out, had fun, and done their best was victorious.

One day the final buzzer of your life will sound, and the question at that moment will be this: Did you allow Jesus to be your coach? Did have faith that He would win the game for you—or are you still trying to win it yourself? It's a question worth contemplating. (2003)

3

On Family

Both the one who makes men holy and those who are made holy are of the same family. *–Hebrews 2:11*

Just Because

I always wondered how my Mom collected children the way she does. Of course, she always wanted kids—lots and lots of kids. Unfortunately, she ended up having only three. Nonetheless, she was never one to cry about what she didn't have, so she poured herself into us and taught us how to love so that people would migrate to us. As they migrated to us, they migrated to her as well. Our friends were her friends. They were as welcome at her house as we were. Plus, they never had to worry about being grounded. And so they came.

First it was our high school friends, who gladly came and ate out with my folks most Saturday nights and then came home with us to play the game of the month—Michigan Rummy, Pictionary, Back-up Three. We stayed up until four in the morning many, many nights fighting for the right card or screaming out things that sounded like something else. Slowly-but-surely, one-by-one Mom collected a few more kids.

Then we went off to college, and the merry-go-round of roommates and friends coming home started. Dances, parties, or just coming home to be home, they came, and she welcomed them all. There was always enough to eat and plenty of room to sleep—even if it was on the floor.

As college days waned, we each got married, and Mom added a few more kids to her collection. Their pictures now grace her walls right along with ours. It wasn't long, and we began having a whole new batch of kids for Mom to love. However, we quickly noticed that she wasn't as tough on them as she was on us. If they spilled something, it could be cleaned. If they left their toys out, they could be picked up. It took another 13 years, but she added ten more "grand" kids to her growing list.

Only then, however, did the exponential compounding interest of her love investments begin kicking in. You see, I'm a lot like her. I welcome people into my home to laugh, to play, and to live. As they began to know me, they eventually met her, and once again the additions started.

The other day one of these as Mom calls them "fate grandkids" showed up at my house. I said, "Oh, Mom and I were talking about you today. She said to tell you that she loves you." The young lady sat for a moment before saying, "And…?" "And nothing. Just that she loves you. Why, is that weird?"

She looked slightly bewildered. "Yeah. It is. No one ever told me they loved me just because before." Finally, I now understand how Mom does it. (2003)

My Father's House

Years ago my Saturday nights were planned long before we ever got to Friday. My friends and I would go to church, go out to eat with my parents and then go to my house for a long night of whatever the game of the season was. We would stay up far into the night playing Michigan Rummy, Pictionary, Guesstures, or Scattergories. More than once a worried parent called to check up on a child and to make sure they were at my folk's place and not up town running around. They were always there around that kitchen table laughing and having a great time.

I don't really remember how the tradition started, or who the first friends I invited over were. However, over the years there was a long line of them. Theresa. Elaine. Kirsten. Lorelea. Michael. Lee. Raymond. Dana. Damian. Mike. Eventually my younger sister's friends joined us, and there were very few Saturday nights that our house wasn't an all-out party.

Now mind you, my parents were always there. In fact, my mom seldom went to bed before everyone left as she was often the last challenger standing no matter what the game was. My dad, on the other hand, had to be up at 5 a.m. on Sunday morning to go out and milk cows. More than once, he rounded the corner at 4:30 in the morning, one eye half-opened to stare at us and ask what we were still doing awake.

We had a lot of good, honest fun in that house, and my friends never balked at going there instead of driving around looking for trouble. It was simply more fun than anything else we could be doing.

Recently I've been looking at my life and realizing that one of my goals is to point as many people to Heaven as I can through my writing and through my life. For awhile it bothered me that maybe I was saying in that goal that I thought I was the one through which they were going to get to Heaven. Of course that wasn't my intent, but there was a nagging thought that maybe that's how it would be interpreted.

It didn't take a genius, but it did take some soul-searching, to realize where that thought came from—Satan, the number one instigator of doubts of all time. Max Lucado once said that "Satan doesn't want to convince us, he just wants to confuse us," and that was certainly true in this case.

It wasn't until I thought back to my high school years and how much fun we had at my parents' house that I finally put all the doubts aside. You see, I don't think I'm the reason they will end up going to Heaven—that is their choice and their business. However, I *am* the one who can invite them. I figure we'll all be better off in Heaven than out on the streets somewhere, so once again, my plan is to invite as many people as I can to join me for a joyous time in my Father's house. It worked once. I hope it works again. (2004)

Faith

In the abyss between life and death resides only faith. Experts call this abyss "Motherhood."

Lying on a cold, hard bed only six months along with my first child, I faced the frightening implications of this truth. With each contraction, my body shook uncontrollably as terror clutched at me. My only lifeline was my husband's hand gripping mine over the abyss as love for life—mine and that of our tiny, still-unseen child's—burned deep in our hearts. One after another after another the nurses piled the bloody sheets into the corner until the doctor pronounced those fateful words, "The baby's coming."

Then, with control slipping past me into a haze of drugs and fear, I made that one, final leap—from control to faith—from childlessness into motherhood.

The next thing I remember was my husband's hand once again holding mine as he said the words that officially changed my life forever, "We have a little girl."

For the next two months images blurred together as ups and downs alternated at break-neck speed. One minute spent holding my two-pound, yet weightless, daughter next to me versus the next three weeks spent holding only tiny fingers through an isolet window—waiting for the next opportunity to get to hold my baby again.

The drugs, powerful enough to keep her safe from infection, again and again blew through her small, fragile veins while all I could do was watch, pray, and hang onto the faith that somehow we would get through this. If we could just make it to the next horizon, through the next transfusion and the next round of drugs, then everything would be all right, then I could live again. Until then, survival was my only goal.

In the darkness of a soul in crisis, my prayers became much deeper and far simpler. No longer was I praying for selfish requests. Now my prayers centered wholly on the tiny baby God had entrusted to my care. The Lord has said, "Cast your burden upon the Lord, and He shall sustain you" (Psalms 55:22), and during those long days and even longer nights, that was all that kept me going.

As simple as that sounds, however, reality was that my only real positives were formed by the negatives: "It's not pneumonia." "It's not an infection." "We won't have to put the IV in her head—this time." The struggle to live was being waged not only by the tiny baby lying helplessly in the incubator, but by her mother's spirit as well. Fear laced every call to the hospital, every question, every conversation. But always the faith remained. Somehow we would make it. Somehow God would sustain us. Somehow...

Then in one faltered heartbeat the negatives became negatives again, and I faced a test of faith even more terrifying than my own journey through the abyss—my baby's journey to the edge of the River Jordan. All her veins had been blown. If a new IV was necessary, it would have to be put in her head—all the other options had been exhausted.

In utter desperation I left the hospital with my husband. On a rain-soaked highway with the amber glow of the streetlights flashing above me, I reached a place that I had never known existed—the place where faith no longer resides.

"Why, God?" I asked the darkness around me. "Why?"

But God has promised, "I will never leave you, nor forsake you" (Hebrews 13:5), and I am here to tell you, He does indeed send messengers to help when you ask. Truth is, even in that moment of despair, my messenger from God was sitting right by my side—exactly where he had been throughout the whole ordeal. Slowly my husband reached over, took my hand, and spoke the words that I would cling to not only for this one night but for the rest of eternity. "She's going to be okay. You've just got to have faith."

It's been five years since that night, but those words will be with me always. Every time I let my baby—big girl now—off at play school. Every time my second daughter lets go of my hand and walks off on her own. Every time one child or the other screams in pain or in fear at two o'clock in the morning—the words come back to me, "She's going to be okay. You've just got to have faith."

In the days to come, the phrase will only become more powerful. During the long nights when the girls fail to call or on the days when they experience their own griefs, the words will be there to help me through. Time and again as I hold my children for one brief moment and then release them into the abyss to live their own lives, the words will be there.

Through school, best friends, boyfriends, first dates, first heartbreaks, in partnership with God and my husband, I will remain the rock on which these two girls can build their lives. Until someday in some beautiful, sunlit church, I will watch from a front pew as they stand before God and pledge themselves to another forever. Then as they turn, kiss me, and walk away into their own lives, the words will be there again. "She's going to be okay. You've just got to have faith."

The day will come, of course, when the abyss will stretch before me again "when Christ, who is our life, shall appear, then shall you also appear with Him in glory" (Colossians 3:4).

In some darkened room on another cold, hard bed, I will step toward the abyss to make my final journey Home. However, this time I will have not one but three sets of hands to hold onto. Then, looking up into the eyes of the two beautiful women my daughters have become, the sadness at our imminent parting will be there, but a greater understanding will hold me also.

Without a doubt, I know that as I slip from the darkness of this world into the light beyond, I will hear that voice one more time: "They're going to be okay. You've just got to have faith." (2000)

Sunday Dinner

No one appreciates mothers enough. In this life, that's a given. The only one who comes closest to a real appreciation is a woman who has become a mother herself, and even she probably doesn't fully appreciate the woman a generation above her.

Where did I come to this conclusion? Sitting in a church pew as the priest extolled the virtues of "Keeping Holy the Sabbath." In the sermon he specifically forbade the parishioners from mowing the lawn, fixing up the house, or doing paperwork on Sundays. He said (and I quote), "Sundays should be a day of rest in which the whole family gathers around the table for Sunday dinner."

Now, during my pre-motherhood days, this sounded like a great idea. You go to church, come home, watch some football on television, then go in and gather around the table for a full Sunday dinner, bow your heads, and have yourself "a day of rest." Notice I said "during my pre-motherhood days."

Throughout my motherhood days, however (which for those of you who don't know that means roughly from the day you give birth until the child buries you), a more accurate picture of "Sunday dinner" is thus:

You've managed to get the kids bathed, dressed, and in the car with only a shoe missing and one coat on upside down.

You get to church and sincerely ask the Almighty to just get you through the parking lot and to a pew before your knees or shoulder gives out from the strain of dragging in the full diaper bag, two sippy cups, an extra blanket and the 20-pound toddler who's squirming to get out of your arms. You make it through the service with the toddler C-THUNKING on the pew ahead of you only enough times to be stared at twice by your fellow parishioners just to make it back home in time for your husband to turn on the game and your kids to started yelling about who did what to whom.

In the midst of minor chaos, you whip something out of the refrigerator, wondering how long it's been in there and if anybody will notice it's been microwaved once it gets to the table. With the toddler clinging to your knees, you manage to put together a somewhat respectable meal—even if it does include chicken nuggets and French fries.

Wishing you had earplugs to drown out the crying of the toddler and the yelling of the others, you get the plates on the table and call everyone to the table for "Sunday dinner." As you referee the current dispute about if one child said they didn't like peas or not the last time, you do manage to get in a few bites before someone thinks of something you forgot... A serving spoon, salt, a fork, water...

A blink and the meal is over. If you're lucky, you will get a "Thanks, Honey" from your husband just before he goes back to the chair for an afternoon nap. Then, I invite you, as you look around at the table strewn with dishes and pans, glasses and silverware, close your eyes, take a deep breath, and say a genuine prayer of thanksgiving for your mother.

I think that may be why God put the "Honoring Your Father and Mother" Commandment just after the "Keep Holy the Sabbath Day" one—because He already knew about Sunday dinner. (2004)

Be Not Afraid

"Let your heart not be troubled, neither let it be afraid." –John 14:27

Fear is one thing. Helpless anxiety is another. Fear brings up your defenses, makes you ready to fight—to take on the aggressor and win. Helpless anxiety, on the other hand, saps every ounce of energy you have because you know that fighting will do no good and nothing you do will make any difference whatsoever anyway. Helpless anxiety wraps around you like a wet blanket. It weighs on you, takes the breath right out of you. It's a horrible place to be in.

That's where I was—wrapped in helpless anxiety—as I sat in the darkened church, feeling empty and alone. My husband sat beside me, holding my hand, but that didn't seem to help. Nor did it change the fact that our baby was six miles away lying in an incubator, fighting for her life. Born three months early, her tiny body was covered in a mass of tubes and wires. Her legs were the size of my husband's finger, and her tiny little hand couldn't even get all the way around my finger.

And I was helpless to do anything to make her better.

Sure, the doctors told me I was lucky that I had taken such good care of myself, that because of my good health, she was developed even beyond the 25 weeks she should have been. But I didn't feel like much of a hero. I felt like I had let down this little one who was counting on me. The should-haves and could-haves ran around in my head constantly bumping into one another and tripping over themselves, fighting to remind me of my guilt. That night, as I listened to what was supposed to be an up-lifting service, I didn't feel very up-lifted. In fact, I felt more depressed than I ever had in my life.

Then the soloist began a song from my past. I knew the words by heart although I wonder now if I had ever really understood them. I tried to sing, to get the words to come out of my mouth, but my heart just hurt too much. So instead of words, tears came as God whispered to me through that song, "Be not afraid. I go before you always. Come follow Me, and I will give you rest."

Be not afraid? How could I not be afraid? Afraid was the only thing I could feel. I wanted to DO something. I wanted to make things better. I wanted to go back and a do a hundred-million things differently so that we wouldn't be standing there praying for my daughter's survival. And yet, here was God telling me not to be afraid.

For the first time since the whole ordeal had started nearly a month before, I cried. I didn't want to, but I couldn't stop the tears from flowing down my cheeks. As they sang about standing before the power of Hell and death being at your side, as they sang about knowing God is with you through it all, I really wished I could feel His presence. I needed that. I guess I did feel His presence through the words of that song. A song that God spoke through another person to me, intended to give me comfort in my hour of greatest need.

In minutes the song was over, and the life went on. I wiped my face, picked up my courage, and marched forward— sincerely hoping God did indeed have a plan in mind, hoping as well that He would be faithful to His promise that He has not given us "the spirit of fear; but of power and love."

Over the course of the next month, slowly but surely my daughter gained weight—one agonizing gram at a time. At one point we even threatened to stuff her diaper with quarters (each one gram) so that she could get to the magic number—1812 grams—4 pounds, so we could take her home. Although at the time it seemed like an eternity, in retrospect it doesn't seem like it took all that long. Two months to be exact. A full month less than the doctors had warned it would take. Then one cloudy September day we got to take our perfectly healthy baby home for good.

Less than a year later, I stood with my baby girl in my arms in that same church, and suddenly that familiar music started once again. "Be not afraid... I go before you always..." I looked down at my beautiful girl, and the tears started rolling once more. Hugging my baby to me, I could only sing with my heart because the tears choked out the words.

Even today seven years and a myriad of scraped knees later, when those notes play together, I am reminded to the depth of my soul that God is indeed here with me. In my most terrifying moments, He is by my side. More than that, He can see the other side to where I can't, and He knows that in that moment things will be all right. And so, as a wise man once said, "All I have seen teaches me to trust Him for all I have not seen."

Because God saw fit to show me, I now understand that we can all "Be not afraid..." (2003)

4

On Others

Where two or three are gathered in My name, there am I in their midst.

--Matthew 18:20

The Red Ribbon

Everyone wants a blue ribbon. Blue. First place. The best. Even kindergarteners want that blue ribbon. In sports, I was never a blue-ribbon person. In a race I was always last. In baseball I was as likely to get hit on the head as to drop the ball. In basketball I was fine as long as there weren't nine other players on the court with me. Where I got my horrible sports ability, I don't know, but I got it. And I got it early.

During the spring of my kindergarten year, our class had a fieldtrip to a park in a town about 20 miles away. Making that drive now is no big deal, but when you're six and you've lived in a town of 300 all your life, going to a town of a couple thousand is a very big deal. Nonetheless, looking back now, I don't remember much of that day. I'm sure we ate our little sack lunches, played on the swings, slid down the slide—typical six-year-old stuff. Then it was time for the races.

However, these were no ordinary races. Some parent had come up with the idea to have the picnic kind of races, like pass the potato under your neck and hold an egg on a spoon while you run to the other side. I don't remember too much about these, but there was one race that will forever be lodged in my memory—the three-legged race.

The parents decided not to use potato sacks for this particular race. Instead, they tied our feet together. One lucky little boy got me for a partner. Now what you have to know about this little boy is that he was the second most athletic boy in our class. I'm sure he knew he was in trouble the second they laced his foot to mine. As for me, I was mortified. This guy was a winner. He almost always won, and I knew that, with me, he didn't have a chance.

However, apparently he didn't realize that as deeply as I did at the time. He laced his arm with mine, the gun sounded, and we were off to the other side. Couples were falling and stumbling all around us, but we stayed on our feet and made it to the other side. Unbelievably when we turned around and headed back for home, we were in the lead! Only one other couple even had a chance, and they were a good several yards behind us.

Then only feet from the finish line, disaster struck. I tripped and fell. We were close enough that my partner could have easily dragged me across the finish line and won. He could have, but he didn't. Instead, he stopped, reached down, and helped me up—just as the other couple crossed the finish line.

I still remember that moment, and I still have that little red ribbon. When we graduated 13 years later, I stood on that stage and gave the Valedictory address to that same group of students, none of whom even remembered that moment anymore. So, I told them about the little boy who had made a split-second decision that helping a friend up was more important than winning a blue ribbon. In my speech I told them that I wouldn't tell which of the guys sitting there on that stage was the little boy although he was up there with me. I wouldn't tell because in truth at one time or another all of them had been that little boy—helping me up when I fell, taking time out from their pursuit of their own goals to help a fellow person in need.

And I told them why I've kept that ribbon. You see to me, that ribbon is a reminder that you don't have to be a winner in the eyes of the world to be a winner to those closest to you. The world may judge you a failure or a success, but those closest to you will know the truth. That's important to remember as we travel through this life.

You may not have a red ribbon to prove it, but I sincerely hope you have at least a few friends who remember you for taking time out from your pursuit of that blue ribbon to help them. I'm thinking those will be the ones that really count—I know it's the one that counted the most to me. (2003)

An Everyday Lesson from a Very Rich Man

Four years ago I wrote an article called, "Living in God's Hands." It was about how God had led me to a seminar by a man who helped me to learn to market on the Internet. The man's name was Corey Rudl. There was so much to talk about in the story at the time I had to skim over the top of it and hit only the high points. It wasn't until this afternoon when I found out with complete disbelief and grief that Corey had died in a car accident that I took the time to remember the rest of the story. And what a story.

You see, I signed up for one seminar that led to a smaller seminar that Corey was giving. At the time I knew it wasn't unusual for Corey to speak to upwards of 1,000 people in a seminar, but this one was to be very small—only about 25 people. So I was excited to say the least, and I was not disappointed. For three hours we sat riveted as Corey strolled around the room, talking at the speed of lightning. By the end of the first three hours I had 12 pages of notes.

At the lunch break I dashed out and down the block, grabbed something quick, and headed back. We had an hour. It wasn't like I had to rush, but I was afraid my car would break down and I would be forced to walk back. I certainly didn't want to miss anything because I was dilly-dallying around.

When I got back, I was the only attendee in the room with about 40 minutes to spare. Corey and his small staff of about four were still working. Unfortunately something in the computer system had gone wrong, and it wasn't working the way Corey wanted it to work. At the time he was worth in the neighborhood of $20 million. In a suit that could've bought a small island, here he was crawling around on the floor under the tables trying to figure out which cord hooked to which thing to fix the glitch.

As this was going on, one of Corey's staff members, Travis came up and started asking me about my experience— why I was there, if I was getting anything out of the seminar, how many pages of notes I had, what kind of books I write, that kind of thing. Every so often, Corey would pop his head up over the table and ask, "Is lunch here yet?"

Apparently the restaurant they'd ordered lunch from was running behind, and as time dwindled down, their window of time to eat was thinning quickly. The "no" would come from the back of the room, and Corey would say "okay" before diving beneath the table again. This is going to sound unbelievable, and thinking back on it now, it is even to me, but while all of this was going on, Corey was asking me questions as well. He was interested to hear how I had found his stuff, what I thought of it as I read it, what things I had already tried, what things I planned to try. There was no end to the questions!

To this minute I don't know how he did it, but he managed to fix that computer. Lunch arrived, and he inhaled a sandwich and fries. With five minutes to spare, he put on his jacket and was waiting with a smile when the other people came back. I'm sure they never knew the chaos that had surrounded him for the better part of an hour. He looked like peace personified.

Yes, Corey Rudl was a very rich man. To me, he was the servant God gave five talents to, who used them, and they multiplied many fold. In fact, if you are reading this now, you can thank Corey for it because I never could have found you on my own. Corey used the talents God gave him to make his own fortune, and then he willingly passed that knowledge onto others. In fact, when he was married a year ago, he invited all of his subscribers to his wedding—for free. I didn't get to go. I wish I could have.

A huge, sad void has been left in the Internet Marketing world with the passing of Corey Rudl into God's Kingdom, and it has nothing to do with the money he helped anybody make. It has to do with the man he was. The man who had enough money to sit back and do nothing for the rest of his life but instead chose to spend his time crawling around on the floor, looking for the cord that wasn't hooked up properly, waiting for lunch that was late, and doing it with a grace and a peace and a kindness that defy human logic.

Yes, Corey was rich, but it had nothing to do with money. I'm grateful for that lesson and wish only that he could've stayed with us longer to teach me more just like it. (2005)

The Five Steps of Forgiveness

In every life there is someone who needs forgiven. There is a father or mother who made mistakes in raising us. There is a teacher who was harsh or uncaring. There is a friend who misused our friendship. There is a boss or co-worker who tried our patience and won. There is a spouse or loved one who damaged us under the guise of love. There is a child who took everything we taught them, then went off and damaged themselves and others in ways we could never have seen. And there is our own worst judgment turned on ourselves. In every life there is someone to forgive.

If you are someone who needs to find a way to forgive, here are the best steps I've found in order to do that (and no, it's not simply, "I forgive you" and the matter is settled. That only works for children who are two).

The first step to forgiveness is to ask God to help you to be willing to forgive. Forgiving someone because everyone else says you should or because you know it's the right thing to do will leave you feeling empty and angry if you try to force yourself to do so. Therefore, you must first ask God for the willingness to forgive. The best way to do this is to say, "God, please soften the hard places in my heart toward _____ so that I can be willing to forgive him/her." Now, this is not a one-time and it's done thing. It may take a few days of saying this repeatedly or it may take a few months if the trauma has been damaging enough or if it was long-lasting. But that is the first step—to be willing.

The second step for some may actually be the first step. They may already be willing to forgive the person, but just not know how. In this step the person trying to forgive simply says, "Lord, help me to forgive _____ for any and all wrongs they have done to me." Again, this step may take some time. I have found that if you will say this every time your thoughts go to that person, sooner or later, your heart will begin to feel forgiveness.

Now many people stop there, and then wonder why later on the forgiven person and the hard feelings surrounding that person don't go away. You think, "I've forgiven them, so why don't I feel better about it? Why is that still bothering me?" It's still bothering you because you haven't completed the forgiveness process.

Sure, you've forgiven them, but what I've learned is that often there were two people in the situation, and you haven't forgiven the other person—you. I had a roommate in college who was like a sister to me for about 18-months. We were all-but inseparable. Then she found a boyfriend. Suddenly the friendship I had invested a lot of time and emotion into changed in a way I wasn't ready for. I was angry and hurt and afraid and lonely. She tried, but our friendship didn't survive.

I knew I had to find a way to forgive her, and eventually I did. But I still felt horrible about the way things had ended. Even after I re-established contact with her and got our friendship to a place where we both knew we were no longer angry and hurt, I still didn't feel right about the whole thing. Then, one day I heard someone say that you need to say, "I forgive myself for ever thinking I ever did anything wrong." I forgive myself... That was the part I had been missing. I had forgiven her, but I had never forgiven myself for the large part I had played in the whole mess.

So, I started, "I forgive myself for ever thinking I did anything wrong with _____." You did what you knew how to do at the time, and as Maya Angelou says, "You did what you knew how to do at the time, and when you knew better, you did better." Slowly over time, my guilt about the situation started to dissipate until now I can look back on that experience and be grateful for the good times and the blessings of the times we had instead of focusing on all the junk at the end.

A few years later I ran up against another life lesson about forgiveness. This time it was with a co-worker who on the outside seemed "lovey-dovey" but who was actually cunning, manipulative, and destructive. Unfortunately because of my position, I was in close contact with this person almost every day. I did my best to remember that she was hurting and that the stuff she did really didn't have to do with me, and generally just tried to stay above the fray. After a year she left the job, and I was elated because I felt I had "passed that test" without getting un-Christian about the things she had done to me.

Over the next several years, I went through the other steps—forgiving her, forgiving myself. However, I still didn't feel totally whole about the situation. Then one day I was thinking about it, and I thought, "You know, I've never prayed to be at peace with what happened." Immediately I started praying, "Lord, please help me to be at peace with this situation and with _____." Eventually I did feel peace.

Shortly thereafter the Lord placed a book in my hands that illuminated the final step of forgiveness. I had forgiven her, I had forgiven myself, I was at peace with the situation... But God doesn't require that we simply "tolerate" people—He says that we should LOVE them. Boy, now that was a hard concept with this person. He wanted me to love her? Odious, would be the word that comes to mind as God and I had that conversation. Nonetheless, I knew He was right.

It was then that I applied the final step. I prayed, "Lord, please help me to love _____." The first few times I just about choked on the words, but the more I said them, the more the feelings of hurt in my heart changed. Slowly something else began to take over. Then I began to really feel love toward this person and to pray for her in a way that I hadn't before.

However, I still wondered if it was real or if it was just an act of my imagination that wanted so much to please God that I wanted it to be real.

Well, as always happens when you ask God a question, He sends an answer. My husband came home one evening, and he had been out on a job replacing some doors. This person came out and started screaming at him about if the old keys would still fit and how were they going to lock the building that night and how the neighborhood thieves would probably make away with anything of value if they didn't get it locked up properly. In short my husband was taken aback and shocked at this exchange. By the time he got home, he was just plain mad. However, until that point he hadn't told me who it actually was.

Then he said, "When she left, she said, 'Tell Staci and the kids I said hello.'" Until she said that, he hadn't even realized who it was. As soon as he said that, I knew, and my suspicions were immediately confirmed when he told me who it was. The strange thing was—in my heart the moment he said her name, there was nothing other than peace. Even as he continued to rant and rave about all the stuff she had said, there was nothing but peace. Finally I said, "You know, it would sure be horrible to have to live life like that. Think about how many people want nothing to do with her and who are excited when she leaves the room. I feel sorry for her. She really needs a lot of prayer."

It wasn't an act. It was honestly how I felt. And that, I think, is real forgiveness. And that, I guarantee you, is the power of the five steps.

Be willing to forgive
Forgive the other person.
Forgive yourself.
Ask for peace.
Ask for love.
It will set you free in ways that you cannot even begin to fathom.

(2004)

Boring Yourself

There are certain things in life that I really wanted to get right—especially those things I knew I would only have one shot at. I don't know why exactly, but I've always lived my life thinking about what I want to be proud of years from now when my grandchildren ask about my life. That may be why I was so unhappy when our senior high school class chose our motto.

To me, our motto was supposed to say something about who we were, about who we wanted to be, about where we were going. It had to be inspirational, up-lifting, and encouraging. In short, it was important to me to get it right. My own motto was the ultra-up-lifting quote by Ralph Waldo Emerson, "What lies behind us and what lies before us are tiny matters compared with what lies inside us." See? Exceptionally inspirational.

So I was mortified when the motto I had nominated (no, almost 15 years later I don't remember what that was) went down in flaming defeat to the motto the rest of the class wanted. The eye-raisingly dubious motto: "Is life not a thousand times too short for us to bore ourselves?"

Now I knew why the partiers in our class chose this saying. I knew what it meant to them, and I was horrified that for the next million years or so, my photo would hang just over this audacious maxim in the high school halls.

However, life has a way of pulling you up short just when you think you've got it all figured out. Nineteen months after our graduation, one of the kids who had fought the hardest for this very motto was killed in a car accident. By all accounts he was by then an upstanding member of our military—busy pursuing a life he had partied too hardy to see in high school.

When I heard the news, I had to think that yes, life was far too short for that young man to have bored himself. Far too short indeed.

Turns out, though, as hard as I fought against having this saying hang under my photo, it is the perfect saying for the way my life has gone as well. There have been very few boring moments since the 23 of us hung that plaque on that wall. Many, many of those moments I've spent frantically trying to keep up, catch up, or get ahead. Very few have been spent sitting around wondering why someone doesn't come do something for me.

Yes, I'm living, and I'm proud I am. I don't have time to be bored. Life's too short. If I forget that, all I have to do is think of my high school class who forced me to understand something about myself that I hadn't even realized was there. I also think about the young man who fought so hard to give me that gift. I will be forever grateful.

I know I will remember that lesson—even when my grandkids ask. So, I guess that's one thing I got right. (2003)

Just A Typical Teenage Boy

Judge not, lest ye be judged. –Matthew 7:1

The call was controversial—just as all really close calls in baseball are. Full speed the runner slid home and thinking he had just scored a game-altering run, he stood up only to face the words, "You're out!"

Now you know how it is when you've given your all to an effort and you stand up, only to hear the ump say, "You're out!" Just running for home when the play could be that close takes confidence and determination, not to mention a certain amount of competitiveness that doesn't just evaporate when you stand up. And it didn't with this teenager either.

Furious, he threw off his helmet and ran over to explain to the ump in no uncertain terms why the call was wrong, why the ump needed glasses, and why he was clearly home and nobody could miss that call so badly. Before his temper really got out of hand, someone pulled him away, and he walked to the bench—livid.

God sees not as man sees...but the Lord looks at the heart. –1 Samuel 16:7

If this first spectacle was all you saw of the matter, don't fret—it was all almost everyone saw. But now, as Paul Harvey would say, "The rest of the story..."

Long after the coaches, players, and fans had gone home, this typical teenage boy realized the impact of his decisions at home plate. Like most of us do when we are faced with the embarrassment of our actions, he could very well have made the logical next choice and just let it slide, reasoning: "Everybody does it. The ump's probably heard that stuff a million times."

However, in the silence of his heart, this young man knew that just because everyone else does it, that doesn't make it all right. And so, long after his buddies had gone home, he tracked that ump back up to the school—not to vandalize his car and not to further harangue him. No, this typical teenage boy tracked this man down so he could tell him face-to-face: "I'm sorry, Sir. I was wrong."

It takes true courage to stand up in the face of those everyday indiscretions we all make and say, "I was wrong. I'm sorry." What makes this apology even more unique is that it wasn't meant for the world to hear, it wasn't meant to make the apologizer look better in the eyes of anyone else. It was meant simply as a way to stay true to his own heart.

In reality the story may well have ended there, and no one would have been the wiser. However, on the way out of town, the ump saw the superintendent and flagged him down to express his appreciation and surprise at the boy's apology. But the ump wasn't the only one who was surprised. The superintendent later talked to the coach to say how impressed he was that the coach had sent the boy to apologize. Only problem: The coach hadn't sent him and knew nothing about the apology until that very moment.

A few days later the coach ran into the boy's father and remarked how impressed he was that his parents had sent the boy to apologize. You guessed it—they knew nothing about it either!

Our truest actions are those that come from the heart—not what someone makes us do because it's the right thing. I know, however, that although the parents didn't intervene on this occasion, they had intervened enough times in the past for this boy to have the ultimate courage to try to remedy a situation when it would have been easier to reason, "He'll get over it."

The truth is at one time or another we have all been this boy—acting out in rage, saying hurtful things, and feeling justified for doing so. The real test comes later when we are presented with the choice to make amends or to walk away thinking, "Ah, they'll get over it."

Maybe the "they'll" is a co-worker, a customer, a friend, a sibling, a child, or a spouse. Whomever it is, don't pass up the opportunity to get right with your own heart. Don't let them walk off the field and drive out of town with you thinking, "Oh, well. No big deal. They'll get over it." The time for apology is now!

Courage is a matter of the heart. I wish that every person in the whole world had the courage of this one typical teenager. If they did, just imagine what "typical" might come to mean! (And a last caveat: The whole world starts with YOU!)

(2003)

Up On the Mountain of Faith

"Help! Help! No help, I'm sliding!"

"You're on skis, Ashley. That's the point."

The poor girl at the top of the line who was headed to the bunny slope lift was scared to death—paralyzed with fear to the point that any tiny move seemed destined to pitch her down the mountain out of control. Her friend seemed not to understand the direness of her situation. To her, skiing was easy. She didn't understand, but I did.

Always longer on doubt and fear than on calm and cool in the sports arena, I understood. Movement on skis seems unfamiliar, unexpected, and dangerous. What seemed like such a fun idea only moments before now seems like the dumbest thing anyone's ever talked you into.

Okay, so even now there are hundreds of people swooshing down the slopes. They obviously know what they are doing. You obviously don't, and so fear takes over. No, not just fear but overwhelming panic that grips your gut and wrenches out small terrified shrieks. This is nuts—craziness. Much better to turn back from this unknown now and go back to the safety of what you do know—life on safe, solid, non-snow-packed ground.

And yet, what Ashley couldn't see at that moment, what she couldn't yet feel is how wonderful it feels to fly, to feel yourself swooping down the mountain with only the wind and the white powder for friends. It's exhilarating, awe-inspiring, life changing. But right there, on the fringes looking in, it just feels like something you'll never be able to do. Something that's destined to kill you if you slide one more inch.

I think that's how a lot of people live life. They see the people who have Jesus in their lives. They see the people who have peace, and it looks so wonderful. Yet they are unsure of how or if to make that decision. Unsure if they can really "do this."

The one thing these people don't need is those Christian "skiers" of us acting like they're silly for feeling like they do. They aren't silly. Their fear is real, and if we don't help them through their fear, they're likely to click those skies right back off and go sit down. Instead of acting superior to them or worse being condescending to their fears, we need get back to the place where we were fearful of taking this giant leap of blind faith and allow them to work through their fear with us at their side.

Undoubtedly in no time at all they will be swooshing down the slopes of faith completely forgetting they were ever afraid of taking that first step. At that point because you have shown them how, maybe, just maybe they'll offer some understanding to another fearful skier along the way home. One at a time, maybe we can get everyone in this fearful world up onto that mountain of faith and skiing through it like a pro.

(2003)

All the Facts

In any given situation, we very rarely have all of the facts—or even enough of them to get angry with someone else. Of course that doesn't stop most of us from getting angry anyway. However, if we can remember the simple truth that maybe we don't know everything, it's amazing what great things God can accomplish when life happens.

The first time God showed me this lesson was when I was teaching high school English years ago. There was one girl in the class who did her level best to make my first year of teaching miserable. Besides the fact that she liked the other English teacher better, I really couldn't find a rational explanation as to why she was so hateful.

However, thankfully, I was secure in my own worth enough that I didn't let it get to me. I just kept thinking, "She must have something really dreadful in her to be able to do that to someone else." Three years later by a mere "God-incidence," I found out that all during that year that young lady was living in a house with a mother whose live-in boyfriend was sexually abusing her younger sister every night in the bed across from hers. Talk about being grateful I hadn't taken the bait and added to the weight she was already carrying.

Going forward that lesson has served me well. When people would do things I thought were obnoxious, unkind or just plain rude, I did my best to remember that I didn't have all the facts and that if I could see their whole situation, it would probably make a lot more sense why they were acting that way.

After I quit teaching to raise my family, I went back to my first love—writing. However, when my first book was published, I soon learned that writing the book was the easy hurdle when compared with promoting a published book. Strapped for time and energy to give to promoting much less to promoting and writing more, I took a friend's advice and started publishing "cyber-serials" through my website. Basically, a cyber-serial is one of my novels, published two chapters at a time, through my newsletter by email, free for anyone who's subscribed to the newsletter. The idea was a hit although at the time I only had about 600 subscribers. People were writing to say how much they liked the book (and then books when the second one started the next year). I felt like God had truly led me to publishing like this—at least for now because it solved so many problems I was having with the other way of publishing.

Then shortly after sending out a set of chapters midway through my second cyber-serial, I got an email back with the same subject it went out with. Figuring it was either an "unsubscribe" or a comment, I opened it. There in brilliant red on black were the two chapters I had just sent out—line edited. That's right. Just like your high school English teacher used to do to your papers when it looked like she had bled all over them!

It took me a full minute to get over the shock. I mean, I'm sure you have found mistakes in books before, but have you ever actually taken out a red pen, marked up two whole chapters, and sent it back to the author so they could see what they were doing wrong?

I finally shook my head in disbelief and clicked off the message, still trying to figure out what to do with it and how anyone would have the audacity to do such a thing. After thinking about it for about three days, I finally decided what possible good would there be in responding or even in getting mad about it although clearly those were options. Someone was obviously trying to take me down a peg—either that, or I just didn't have all the facts.

A month went by, and it was time to send out the new chapters. About two hours after I did, I got a new message from this same person. Figuring I would find another set of marked up chapters, I opened the email, which started something like:

"Dear Staci, I am soooooo, sooooooo sorry! I really REALLY messed up! When you sent me the chapters last month, I thought they were chapters from my critique group! I was new to the group, and although I had never done anything like that before, I thought I needed to really do a good job editing because I didn't want them to think I didn't know what I was talking about. I am so very, very sorry! Can you ever forgive me..."

It went on thus for about a page and a half. As I read it, I just started laughing! It took another 20 or so messages between the two of us before she finally quit telling me how sorry she was and asking my forgiveness. It seems not only was she not comfortable with critiquing, she also felt horribly guilty when she even inadvertently hurt someone's feelings, which she was sure she had done with her critique of my chapters.

Funny thing though, after getting to know her and finally coming to the point where we could *both* laugh about it, I then asked her if she would really review my next cyber-serial when I got ready to publish it. It took her awhile to realize that I was serious, but she finally agreed.

Shortly thereafter I received one of the most glowing reviews I've ever gotten. In fact, she called it "one of the three best books I've ever read." Now you might think she was saying that out of guilt. I wondered that, too; however, based on the in-depth analysis I did by asking her direct questions about different aspects of the book, I don't think so. I think she genuinely liked the book.

More than that, she started asking about how I wrote the way I did, and I started trying to explain it. Emails flew back and forth on the subject as we became friends. A couple of times throughout the rest of the year, a message from her would pop up into my inbox. "Just wondering when you are going to print-publish 'Princess.' When you do, I want a copy." I always just laugh and tell her God's got my priorities in a different place right now—at home with my kids. So I'm not print-publishing anything at the moment, but it's nice to know she liked the book that much.

I consider this woman a true friend now, but I often think how off-track that friendship would've gone had I jumped to anger without stopping to remember that I didn't have all the facts. It's a lesson I'm glad I learned early because I got a really good friend out of a simple mistake I'm sure the Devil meant to use to tear us both down.

These things happen. It's life. But I'm here to tell you, it pays God-dividends to remember that in any given situation, you don't know all the facts.

(2004)

The Glass House

...Excerpt from "Dreams By Starlight" by Staci Stallings...

"Fragile Glass"

It was the beginning of the rough draft of Camille's analysis of Laura from "The Glass Menagerie."

"In a world of glass houses, it may take only one, small stone to bring a life down, to crumble it to the core, to shatter the hopes and the dreams of someone with only hopes and dreams to live on. It may be a simple laugh, hurled at someone at her most vulnerable moment. It may be a comment, a thoughtless aside, meant to be funny but actually so devastating that the object of it never really recovers. Or it could be a parent's expectations set so high that no mere mortal could ever reach them, and then hurled with every opportunity at the fragile glass the child has constructed. Whatever it is, the stone seldom matters to the person hurling it, but to the person on the receiving end, it could be all it takes to destroy a house, painstakingly constructed, and meant only to shelter a lost, hurting soul from a cold, cruel world of stone throwers."

(2000)

5

On Death

So we fix our eyes not on what is seen, but on what is unseen. For what is seen is temporary, but what is unseen is eternal. –2 Corinthians 4:18

A Stop on the Road of Life

With three kids, a business, a husband with a business, a house, a yard, and a very close extended family, my time is at a premium. This means I'm usually running as fast as I can to keep up with everything—and sometimes failing miserably in that endeavor. Recently I was caught between two major obligations, driving from one to the other, and late again.

In my mind I was ticking off all that had to be done when I got home: make supper, give the kids a bath, help with homework, straighten the house, lay out clothes for the morning... when suddenly the pickup in front of me put on his blinker and veered over to the empty lane beside us. I hit the brakes and then realized why he had stopped. A funeral procession.

Instantly although my first thought was, "Oh, no! I don't have time for this!" I, too pulled to the side of the road, turned off my radio and stopped just as the policeman and the hearse passed. I looked beyond them to see how many cars with lights there were and realized I was going to be there for a while.

Turns out, I had no idea how long "a while" would be. Because the procession was actually coming around a corner up the road, I couldn't actually see the whole thing, which could easily have been 200 cars or more. Nonetheless, as I sat there in silence, perspective began to fall around me. Here we on this side of the road were, living our lives, driving in the fast lane to get what we had to get done, seeming to have no time as it was, but when we needed to—out of courtesy or obligation—we stopped.

Life stopped so that we could all take a moment to recognize not only the grief of one family, but so that we could recognize that we, too, will one day be at the head of that funeral procession.

See, death and 24-hours, are the two great equalizers in this lifetime. We each have 24-hours to live our lives each day. You cannot buy more time. You cannot will more time. You cannot even strong-arm more time. You and the wino on the street have exactly the same amount of hours in every day. The only difference is in how you choose to use that time. However, here is a sobering thought—you and the greatest doctor on the earth also have the same number of hours in each day. He has used his brilliantly. How have you used yours?

Death is our other greatest equalizer. No matter who you are, where you are from, who you know, or how much money you have, one day you, too, will be laid out and leading that procession. The question is, how long will your procession be?

As I watched this person's procession, it became clear how this person had chosen to use those 24-hours a day that God had granted. Well. Very, very well indeed. The cars just kept coming and kept coming, rounding that bend and lining up until there was a mile of them, and they were still coming.

For one moment that day I stopped on my harried trek through life to really consider where I'm going on this road we call life, what it all means, and whether or not I'm head in the direction that I want to end up. Truth is, it was well worth the stop.

(2003)

Where Were the Angels?

"This light is entrusted to you to be kept burning brightly
. . ." so said the priest the day he handed the baptismal candle to
the parents.

These particular parents were the kind who took that
admonition to heart. They were there for that child. It was
evident in his demeanor and his caring about others. His friends
would say not that he was given a light, but that he was that
light.

Then one Saturday night, the unthinkable. Five days shy
of his sixteenth birthday, on a lonely stretch of country road, he
and three friends drove headlong into the place where the
margin of error is zero.

The pickup flipped once, then twice, and when it finally
came to rest, his flame had left this world. In overflowing tears a
community grieved, for this child was a likeable child, this child
was one of those "low maintenance" ones—the kind that are just
fun to be around, this child was truly a light to his family and to
his peers. And now his light had been extinguished.

Like most kids his age, this young man's life had held so
much promise. He was going to play second base next year for
the baseball team. He was going to get a car for his birthday. He
was going to go back to a wedding dance that night and party
with his myriad of friends. But in one heart-wrenching instant

the flame of his life, of his potential, was snuffed out leaving in its absence only grief, pain, and emptiness.

On the way to the wake service my dad heard the "inspirational story" of a family of five who had all survived a harrowing van rollover with nary a scratch. The radio announcer said, "They were lucky to have their guardian angels in that van that day." Now most of the time, he would have said, "Yeah, they were." Instead my dad, the baseball coach, who had just watched his future second baseman lift up from second base in a Lifestar helicopter only to return in a coffin, said, "I just kept thinking where were the angels that night? Where were this child's angels?"

That question stuck in my mind. As that pickup flipped once, bounced into the air, and dislodged him from his seat—where were the angels at that moment? When the pickup again sailed through the air on its second pass over—why did the angels hang back? Why didn't they rush in to hold this boy, this light, inside the cab? Why did they allow him to be thrown so that his bright, shining flame would burn no more? Why?

At the funeral the same priest who had first presented that light to the parents those few short years before stood before us again with this explanation. "God allowed his own Son to be tried, wrongly convicted, sentenced to death, hung on a cross, and crucified. He could've saved Him, but if He had, the suffering of this world would still extend to the next. At times like this we don't understand why, but we have to understand that 'why' backward means 'Your Holy Will.'"

I had never had cause to think about this scene before—the one with Christ hanging from the cross while the angels hung by and watched. However, later putting the two pieces together, I realized where the angels were. It wasn't that they weren't there. They were simply on the other side of that temple curtain—the one that split down the middle at the moment of Christ's death.

And from that side, they were waiting with open arms to receive and comfort the light that had been sent to this earth for a short time, now destined to return to God's loving embrace.

Where were the angels that evening as the pickup flipped in the air? They weren't far—they just didn't have the mission we would've liked for them to have that day. Yes, bad things happen, and we don't always understand. However, our mission is not to understand—our mission is to believe that in God's plan, not in ours, the angels are always exactly where they are supposed to be.

(2002)

6

On Money

Whoever loves money never has money enough; whoever loves wealth is never satisfied with his income. This too is meaningless. – Ecclesiastes 5:10

Are You Rich?

Are you rich?

Stop. Think about that question for a moment, and answer it honestly. Let it wind down through your head, past your heart and into your soul. Put it into first person.

Am I rich? Ask, and wait for the answer. It's important to get an answer because your whole life is currently being controlled by that answer. Everything you do is colored by it. Every single facet of your life is shaped by it in some way.

In this life there are four answers, and each answer shapes the reality of the person answering in ways they may not even be aware of.

The first group says, "Of course I'm rich. Look at all the money I have." And then they go home to empty houses filled with all the finest things in life but devoid of anything even nearly approximating love. These are the people who are lost but don't know it, or who can't face how barren their lives really are.

The second group says, "I'm not rich. Look around. I can hardly pay my bills each month. I have no savings, my car just broke down, and I have no idea how I'm ever going to send my kids to college." These people hold "poverty" up like a badge of honor when in reality, their focus on the bad keeps them in perpetual bad without any hope of getting to the good in life.

The third group says, "No, I'm not rich because even if I have a lot now, something terrible could happen tomorrow, and then where would I be?" These are the people who are just waiting for bad to happen. They can't enjoy what they do have for fear of the future. So, no matter how much they have now, fear is their dominant emotional state, and it effectively negates any positive feelings making them perpetually feel "poor"— effectively keeping them in bad.

And then there is the fourth group.

The first time I read this question, my resounding answer all the way to the bottom of my spirit was, "Yes, of course I'm rich!" However, it wasn't until a few minutes later that I really thought about the question in terms of money. I simply looked out to where my children were playing as I sat on the steps of my home waiting for my husband to come home, and I said, "Yes." How, in that context, could I answer anything but yes?

Life, however, is not nearly as logical as it sometimes seems. A few days later I asked the question of someone in exactly the same situation, and that person's immediate and resounding response was, "No!" I was astounded. How could the two of us in as close to the same boat as two people can get respond so differently?

The more I reflected on that paradox, the more I learned about how and why I relate to my world the way I do. When I was younger, a friend told me, "You know, you are so lucky. Everything always works out for you." At the time I said, "Yeah, and I work darn hard to make sure it does."

In light of this new question, however, I can see why things work out for me—because I believe that they will and I focus all my energy toward that end. Then, even when they don't work out like I planned, I see that how they worked out was even better than what I had planned or at least exactly the way they were supposed to work out for my continued growth. An understanding which causes me to feel even richer than before.

World-renown motivational speaker Anthony Robbins has an exercise where first you "hope" something will work out.

He says that when you hope, you see two possibilities: the thing working out, and the thing not working out. Then he invites you to "expect" that something will work out. Expecting focuses all of your attention, all of your energy, on the goal being accomplished with no thought to it not working out. When you expect consistently, your goals, your dreams, and your plans have no choice but to come into being because your thoughts create your reality.

And so back to our original question. Are you rich?

When you look at your life, do you expect things to work out? Do you focus all your energy on things working out? Or do you sit back and hope that somehow they will? If your answer to the last question is, "Yes," then I'd be willing to bet your answer to the first is, "No." It's simple—if all your focus on is how "poor" you are, no matter how great things may be, you will find a way to feel "poor."

Sarah Ban Breathnach, best-selling author of *Something More*, suggests keeping a gratitude journal where every day you write down five things for which you are grateful. This is an excellent way to force your mind to focus on answering a resounding, "Yes!" to "Are you rich?" Take a moment, right now, and list ten things in your life for which you would not take a million dollars.

Having trouble thinking of something? Then start with your health—that's an asset most of us take for granted. "But I have a bad back and migraine headaches and PMS," you say. Maybe, but I have an uncle who is stricken with MS, and he literally cannot reliably move any muscle in his entire body. Not only is he in a wheelchair, he must be strapped to that wheelchair so he won't fall out. He cannot feed himself, dress himself, or go to the bathroom by himself. He cannot drive, hold a pencil, type, or even roll over in bed at night under his own power.

Now, how thankful are you for your health? More importantly, are you rich?

In the book *Princess*, by Jean Sasson, a Saudi Arabian princess who on the outside lives a life of luxury and opulence that most of us could only dream about, describes life for women that closely resembles absolute hell. Women locked in lightless rooms for years on end because they brought "dishonor" to the family. Women drowned by their fathers in their family's swimming pool while their mothers and sisters look on helplessly. Young girls sold by their parents, stripped naked, and then bought at auctions by men who want to increase their harems.

And we complain about a bad hair day.

Think about the opportunities and the options you have stretched before you. Yes, you may be in a dead end job or in a dead end relationship, but you don't have to stay there. You can get out. So ask yourself right now, what do you want to do with your life? What is your dream? If you could be anywhere in this life, where would you be? Picture that place in detail. What does it look like? Breathe. Close your eyes, and see it.

If you believe you are rich; if in your soul your answer is a solid, no-questions-asked, resounding "Yes!", then you can achieve that dream and any other dream you focus on. Nothing can stop you.

Now, I can hear some of you saying, "But I'm not rich. Look at all these bad things that have happened to me." Then I say, start a grateful journal today—this very minute. You don't have a second to waste.

Motivational speaker, Marianne Williamson says, "There is nothing holy about poverty." God, the maker of all things, has given you the greatest gift of all—life, but what do most of us do? Sit around complaining about every little thing that has ever gone wrong and whining about how hard this life is.

Let this be your warning: Do not tell your brain you are poor, for when you do, no amount of riches—monetary or otherwise—will ever be enough to make you rich. Believe you are rich, feel you are rich, focus on how you are rich every single moment of every single day. For when you feel you are rich and believe you are rich, more riches will be granted to you.

So, now, let me ask you once more, are you rich? Be careful. The answer is shaping more than you think. (2001)

Selling Him Out for Thirty Pieces

"And he threw the pieces of silver into the sanctuary and departed; and he went away and hanged himself." --*Matthew 27:5*

One thing I love about the apostles is how like us they all were. There was Peter stepping out in faith until he remembered those waves. There was Thomas steadfastly holding to the belief that because it had never been done before, it certainly couldn't have happened now. And then there's Judas—the betrayer. The one who threw away Heaven itself for thirty pieces of silver.

Now I don't know why he made the initial decision, but I'm guessing it went something like this, "Look how much stuff everyone here in Jerusalem has, and here I am with dusty feet following a guy who might actually be lying to all of us for all we know. Okay, at first I believed him, but come on, he's been making some pretty wild claims lately. Besides do you know what I could do with thirty pieces of silver? Why I could start my own business right here in Jerusalem. Then I'd surely be set for life."

It sounded so easy. Just tell the high priests where Jesus was, take the money, and run. It sounded so easy—until Judas realized what he had done. By that time it was too late to go back and change his mind. By that time Jesus had been beaten bloody and sent away to face Pilate. Judas tried to change his mind. He tried to give the ill-gotten money back, but the chief priests wouldn't hear of it. They had what they wanted in the bargain, and they really didn't care how Judas felt about it or what he did with the money.

For a moment suspend your judgment of Judas in the "how could he do that to JESUS?" corners of your mind. Suspend it long enough to ask, "Where in my life am I doing the exact same thing?"

Maybe it's in the time you spend working at night, all the while yelling at your children to be quiet so you can "get something done." Maybe it's selling your soul to the office, fighting to get one more rung up the ladder. Maybe it's selling a product you don't believe in just to make a profit. Maybe it's selling out your co-workers to make yourself look better. Maybe it's out-right dishonesty, taking things that aren't yours.

The story of Judas should serve as our caution that selling God out for a few pieces of silver will not work in the end. Sooner or later you will come to regret what you did, but at that point it will be too late. The devil will only laugh as you fling the money back at him and flee from the temple.

The only way to make sure it's not too late is to make a different decision right now. Resolve not to sell out Jesus and all He stands for in return for a few pieces of silver. The silver will never be worth the cost. Judas found that out, and he hung himself. You've just found it out, and I challenge you to take that understanding and make positive changes in your life. Start focusing on how you can serve the King instead of how you can make a few bucks.

You never know, you may actually gain Heaven in the process!

(2003)

7

On Lessons Learned

I will instruct you and teach you in the way you should go; I will counsel you and watch over you. –Psalm 32:8

Are You At Peace?

Everyone is working so hard these days. Getting ahead—that's what most people call it. We've got cell phones, palm pilots, laptops, beepers, and pagers so that we never have to be disconnected from the world. In fact, there's one commercial that shows a man sitting on a mountaintop next to a pristine lake in the middle of nowhere working on his laptop! The tagline says something like: Keeping you connected no matter where you are.

It's a nice idea really—being connected to our fellow beings on the planet all the time, being able to contact practically anybody anywhere any time. In theory it's a nice idea, but in reality, I think that all this busyness is really a mask for something deeper. Being able to "reach out and touch someone" can easily begin to take over every waking hour so that you increasingly do not have time to get in touch with yourself. And that's a problem.

In her book, *A Return to Love*, Marianne Williamson talks about goals, but she doesn't jump on the "how-to and why-to" bandwagon that most inspirational authors do. What she says instead is that rather than praying for and focusing our energy on attaining goals that we've set, we should pray for and focus on being at peace no matter what happens.

She's not saying, "Sit on your tail, and do nothing." What she's saying is that because we inhabit such a small speck of this immense universe, we cannot possibly know what is truly best in a given situation. For example, say you want a job with XYZ Company, and you truly believe this job will make you happy—that it is the perfect job. So you pray really hard every night that you will get this job, and you do affirmations 100 times every night, "I will be hired by XYZ Company. I will be hired by XYZ..."

Chances are, because of the power of the mind, you will be hired by XYZ Company. However, as often happens, a year down the road you're miserable and you wish you had never heard of XYZ Company. Why? You got the goal. You got what you wanted. You got what you thought would make you happy. But you missed the opportunity to get what you really wanted, and that was peace about the situation of wanting to work for a great company.

You thought that getting *that* job would give you peace and happiness, and now you think you were wrong. Have you ever heard the saying, "Be careful what you ask for because you just might get it"? This is the lesson that saying is talking about. You are asking for what you think will make you happy instead of asking God to make you happy no matter what.

Grasping and truly implementing this lesson requires letting go and letting God take over. Trust to the nth degree. It is embodied in the saying a wise friend once told me: "In the end it will always be okay. If it's not okay, it's not the end."

So, pray for peace in your life. You never know. You just might get what you ask for.

(2003)

The Force and the Dark Side

I don't know if anyone will ever read this for the simple fact that I'm not sure I can corral my thoughts enough to be comprehensible, but here goes...

Upon watching the final installment of George Lucas' *Star Wars: Revenge of the Sith*, it struck me how similar in theme it was to Mel Gibson's *The Passion of the Christ*. Now stay with me here. I'm not totally insane. You see, in The Passion, Christ faces a decision. Will it be worth it to stay true to His soul and His God even if that means losing His physical life in order to save everyone He loves (us) from the power of evil? In *Revenge of the Sith*, Anikan, too, faces a decision. Will it be worth it to trade his soul and maybe even his life to evil in order to save someone he loves? The goal is the same—to save those you love. The paths couldn't be more different, nor could the outcomes.

It is said that the devil doesn't have to convince you, all he has to do is confuse you to throw you off track. This idea is played out masterfully in Revenge. Anikan is pulled in different directions by nearly everyone—the Jedi Knights, Padme, and especially Darth Sidious/the Chancellor. The Chancellor uses his time with Anikan to float trial balloons of confusion into the young man's mind—some good (a way to save Padme), some bad (the Jedi are dishonorable), some just plain confusing (they have asked you to spy on me, haven't they?).

Plagued by nightmares of losing the one he loves and not at all sure where the truth or anyone's real motives lie, Anikan listens to the Chancellor just enough to let himself become confused. Is the Dark Side he's always heard about really dark, or is it just something you can play for a while and then turn from when you want? Can you use it for your benefit and not have it infiltrate your soul? I believe it is Anikan's original intent to do just that—use the Dark Side enough to gain what he wants and then go back to the life of honor. Of course, it doesn't work that way.

Nonetheless, I believe Padme at the end when she says, "There's still some good in him." There is. But his mind has been twisted to the point that he can't figure out what's good and what's bad. He can't figure out who to believe and why. The Jedi are suspicious of him for reasons neither they nor he can really explain. The Chancellor is offering him the power to save the one he loves. The Jedi are saying, "You are not to love anybody." The Chancellor is asking him to spy. Padme is begging him to make everything right. Even the Jedi Knight he looks up to and respects the most, Obi-Wan, unknowingly adds seeds of distrust and confusion into the young man's mind by asking him to spy on the Chancellor and then showing up on Padme's ship. By the middle of the movie, even the watcher in the seats is confused. Whom to believe? Whom to trust? Whom to turn to because no one seems wholly without motive to use Anikan as nothing more than a pawn?

Why did this happen? How did Anikan get stretched in so many different directions? Because he allowed himself to listen to the evil singing so sweetly in his ear in the first place, and because he stopped listening to the Force altogether.

As he stood with the light sabers on either side of Count Dooku's head, he listened to the Chancellor telling him that killing someone would be all right. He went against all his Jedi Knight training—the teachings of the Force. In that moment, he gave in to the desire for revenge and the hatred he had for

Dooku, and in the split second that Dooku's head was removed from his body, Anikan turned his allegiance to the Dark Side. Instantly he is confused. Instantly he says, "What have I done? That's not the way of the Jedi." And the Chancellor smiles with insidious delight. Anikan has taken the first step to the Dark Side.

With that killing on Anikan's conscience, the Chancellor can now twist and turn the knife any way he wants it to go. Thus, Anikan becomes first a confused and then a willing pawn in the cruel and evil web of deceit spun by the Chancellor.

To make matters worse, Anikan believes he has to do it all on his own. He trusts no one, save Padme, and even she has to drag every bit of information about what was really going on out of him. He wraps himself in his own understanding of the world, which was really very limited, and he makes the decision that his power is enough. To further this already unwise aim of doing it by himself, he seeks to know more about the Force and the Dark Side. In other words, he wanted to taste of the knowledge of good and evil. He wanted to play God. No. He wanted to be God. He wanted to be able to give Padme back her life if his nightmares came true. Rather than trusting in the Force, he convinced himself that the Force could not help him. He had to help him. He was on his own.

And so by the advice of the Chancellor that in order to be powerful enough to bring Padme back to life, he had to grab power however and wherever he could, Anikan began to do just that. Thus, with a baby of his own on the way, he walks in and wipes out a small army of unarmed Jedi younglings. If he is to wipe the Jedi out, it is important that he pull the order up from the roots to ensure that the Jedi will be no more. He accomplishes this by killing all of the younglings that would one day become Jedi Knights.

This scene also holds deeper a truth in that up until this point, everyone Anikan has killed is someone unlike himself, someone old, some enemy outside himself, or someone he has convinced himself was an enemy. However, when the lead youngling steps out from behind the council chair, this child very much resembles Anikan as a child. Physically they are very similar, but more importantly emotionally they are similar. Out of all the younglings, this one appears to be the leader. He steps out, and the others follow. He is the one who addresses Anikan with the plea that they are afraid because everyone has left—embodying of course Anikan's own struggles as a child when his mother died and he was abandoned. However, Anikan in his by now all-consuming hatred and fury ignites his light saber to kill this youngling, which so symbolizes the killing of his own innocence. With that deed, he kills any hope he has of ever going back. What follows is a rampage that gets ever more vicious with each passing scene. He continues to annihilate other Jedi Knights who let him in thinking him their friend. But he is no longer anyone's friend—least of all his own.

The more he kills, the more horrific his features and heart become and the more heartless and cruel his actions become. With his innocence gone, he is no longer confused about his turn to the Dark Side. He embraces it full on and begins to believe it really will lead to everything he has so wanted in his life—safety, security, power, pride—until finally he meets again with the one he loves, the one whom he has done all this power-grabbing to save. And what happens? She senses the terrible change that's come over him. She sees what embracing the Dark Side has done to him, and although it breaks her heart to leave him, she cannot live with the evil he has become.

So here he is. He has done all of this for her, and she rejects him. Of course by now he thinks he can make anyone do anything he wants, so in his anger, he puts a death grip on her. Struggling to free herself, Padme finds she cannot get out of his clutches until Anikan's old master, Obi-Wan steps in and saves her just before she is killed.

By this point Anikan has so turned his soul to the Dark Side that even Padme's love and life means nothing to him. If she is not willing to love him, than he does not love her. It is an action born of hurt and fear, but it exacts a toll on her body that will ultimately ensure her death. Translated: Anikan's total embrace of the Dark Side convinces him that exacting revenge on Padme is within his rights because he's mad at her. The Dark Side has so blinded him that he can kill even the one he professed to love, thus forever locking the grip that hatred and fear and torment will have on his soul from that point forward because he could kill even her.

Of course there ensues the epic battle between Obi-Wan and Anikan in the lava pit that to me verily reeked of hell itself. In fact, just prior to Anikan shaking Padme lifeless in a death grip, he tells her that they can stay here and rule over "All of this." (Great idea. Just where I want to stay and raise my kids.) I wonder if he realizes as she is backing away that he made a wrong turn somewhere on the road. If he does realize that, the realization is quickly consumed with his anger at her backing away in horror. In fact, you can almost see it in his grotesquely evil glare. "No, I didn't make a wrong turn. You did, and now you're going to pay."

In the end Anikan is burned by the hell he has chosen. How did his choices lead him here? They led him here because not only did he steadfastly refuse to let go of anything, he also refused to trust anyone other than himself.

The Jedi said he could not wed. He wed anyway. The Jedi said to be patient and wait for his time to become a Master. He didn't want to wait. He wanted that distinction now. At every turn, Anikan chose himself over the Force. At every turn, he relied on his own understanding of the situation, rather than on listening to the Force. In short, choosing the Dark Side is choosing to rely on oneself, to hang onto everything you can possibly grab, to deem everyone else expendable in your quest for what you want—however noble it seems at the time. That's the insidiousness of the Dark Side. It sounds so good and right when it's whispering sweetness in your ear.

Now contrast this tragedy with the triumph of Christ in *The Passion*. Throughout that movie, the things Christ loves the most are stripped away. He loses his friends because they run away. He loses his freedom. He is in shackles and chains. He loses his body as it is ripped, torn, and shredded. He loses the love of people he had cured and healed. He loses his strength as he is forced up Calvary under the burden of the cross. He loses his clothing to the soldiers and his dignity to the wind. In the end he even loses the one he loves the most in this world—his mother. He gives her into the care of someone else, loving her and wanting her to be safe even if he couldn't be there to see to that. And he lets them all go with the heart-wrenching understanding that they were never his in the first place.

In that film, Christ gave up everything, even his life for the love of everyone, even those who hated him so fiercely. More to the point, He surrendered absolutely everything to God. Why? Because at every turn, he refused to listen to the evil one whispering lies into his ears. He refused to rely on his own strength, instead He repeatedly called out to God for strength. He didn't try to do it on his own because he knew he couldn't. He didn't cry out to understand more about why they were intent on killing him. He didn't thirst for the knowledge of good and evil. That didn't matter. He thirsted for God and only God. He chose the tree of life. The tree that ensures that God is with you no matter what horrible events the world throws at you.

Anikan chose the tree of the knowledge of good and evil. He chose to rely on himself, and because he bought into the lie that he could do it himself, he lost everything. He lost the life he had been building. He lost Padme. He lost his very soul. That choice is what turned him into Darth Vadar. Choosing yourself is the way to the Dark Side. Choosing to rely on yourself is the Dark Side. Why? Because in the fog of now, it's too easy to get confused. In the smoke and mirrors of who said what to whom when, truth and right get really hard to find. And confusion is the devil's first line of offense. If he can get you confused, he's got a much better shot at taking you down a road you really don't want to be on.

The solution, if you haven't figured it out already, is to put your life into the hands of Someone who sees the whole situation for what it really is and let Him (God/The Force) make your decisions. This Someone not only sees the pieces of the puzzle you can't see, He sees into the very heart of each and every one of the players. He knows when you're taking a wrong turn, when you are listening to the wrong person, and if you're listening to Him, He will lead you back onto the path of right. He sees it all with perfect clarity. And even when the journey leads through the valley of death, He is at your side at every step. So, the question is: Are you listening to Him, like Christ did, or are you wallowing in your own pit of the knowledge of good and evil trying desperately to figure it out for yourself? Be careful that choice. One side leads to the resurrection and Heaven itself. The other leads to a hell of unmentionable proportions.

(2005)

Life Lesson: Be-Do-Have

This revelation hit me the other day while I was listening to a cassette on having financial balance in your life. On the tape, the author talked about a goal setting seminar he went to. The lesson he was revealing is that too often when we set goals, we are setting the "have" part of the equation, then "doing" the work of getting to the goal without ever making the effort to "be" anything.

If you're paying attention, there's a math lesson that translates to this message. Any math person will tell you that there is a definite order to life. A + B = C, and if you get it out of that order, even the simplest of ideas can get overwhelmingly confusing. So this equation must begin with "be" not "do" or "have."

For example, people set a goal of meeting the right person. That is the "have" that they want, so they begin "doing" the things the world says makes sense to do to get to that goal. They go to bars, they go to church, they go to work, they go to parties, they go to school—all with the spoken or unspoken intention of acquiring what they do not have, a partner. Years ago they called the females with this mindset, "Mrs. Majors."

They were not in college to get a degree; they were in college to get a husband.

In today's world some of these types—men and women—have the "have" and "do" parts down to a science. One manifestation of this is the book, "The Rules." This book purports to explain exactly what you have to "do" to get the goal of "having" a mate. The problem is that this is completely senseless when you understand the equation of "be-do-have."

When you truly get this life lesson, it will have a profound impact on every aspect of your life. No longer will you focus solely on the goal—now you will focus on who you must first become, and the attainment of the goals will follow.

I know, it sounds Pollyanna. It sounds so simple. But it's the simple-sounding things that are often the most difficult to actually do. I see this turmoil in teenagers a lot. They think that their identity is created by who they are with, what they wear, what their outward appearance is. The reality, however, is that identity is based on who you are.

That's why you hear of 10- and 20-year high school reunions in which the popular kids are now struggling and some of the most unpopular kids are now the successful adults. When you understand this equation, it makes perfect sense. Think about it. In high school, the "popular" kids already "have." They have the status, the good looks, the admiration of others. Why work for something you already have?

The unpopular kids on the other hand are forced to find their true identity not in the outer world, but in the inner world. So they work on themselves rather than on what the outside world says is important. Thus, 10 or 20 years down the road, they who have been forced to "be" are now "doing" and "having" in much greater proportion than those who "had" everything.

To be sure, this is a vast generalization. There are popular kids who take time out to work on themselves and "become," and there are unpopular kids who want to "have" so badly that they contort who they are trying to fit in. The exceptions are there, but so is the rule.

You have to be before you can do, and you have to do before you can have. If you don't, nothing you ever get will be enough. And if you do, whatever you have will be plenty. With this in mind, find some time today to fit a little "being" time into your "to-do" list. It may just turn out to be the best time investment you could ever make.

(2002)

Let Go

Although there are a lot of careers in this life that could teach someone to let go, I think that writing has to be near the top of that list. Maybe that's because I write, or maybe that's because it really is. Whatever the case, this understanding was made clear recently when a writer friend of mine asked the question, "How could I not see the holes in my manuscript that my critique partners caught and pointed out? They were so glaring."

As a writer, I completely understand the frustration in this statement. If you are a high school writer only, you may not. While teaching I saw plenty of high school writers. They wait until the last conceivable moment to start, write down everything they can think of on the topic at hand in no particular order, then race to the teacher's desk to fling the paper at her, hoping it's good enough for passing. These people are not the writers of which I speak.

I'm speaking about the writers who think all the way through every word they put down, who cross out, delete, rewrite, re-think, edit, re-edit, and hone every inch of a manuscript before they let anyone else so much as hear the idea presented in it. These are the writers who research until their eyes bleed, think until their brain hurts, and generally torture themselves over every single word because it doesn't just need to be "good," it needs to be "perfect."

Then after they can see no other place in the entire work of oh, say 80,000 words, they heave a sigh of relief and acquiescence and place it into the hands of someone else to read. In high school, these are the kids who have been finished with the first draft of their 250-word essay 40 minutes before the bell rings, but who are still crossing things out and rewriting them even as they slide toward the teacher who's saying, "That's it. Turn in your papers."

It's painful for them to turn their work over to someone else. It's like a mother leaving her first baby with a sitter for the very first time. They hope and pray the reader will be gentle. They hope that when the paper is returned, there are very few red marks if any at all. And above all, they hope they haven't made any grievous errors that will make the reader think they are a complete imbecile who should never have been given a pen and paper in the first place.

This is the kind of writer my friend was and then came the shocker. She had missed something, and not just something but a huge gaping hole in the story and how she told it. When that happens to a writer of this ilk, devastation sets in like a hurricane across a soul. Even the mildest criticism is like a knife to the gut. Immediately after the devastation blows through, the rains of doubt begin to pour. "Maybe I'm not supposed to be a writer. Maybe I just don't have what it takes to do this."

To some extent there might not be a way around this feeling totally; however, I don't think it is completely inevitable. You see, I have found a way (not foolproof but pretty close) to weather this storm and let the manuscript grow as God intended it to. It's called, "Let Go."

That's the short version of having a "Leave Everything To God Opportunity." These types of opportunities are all around us. They are in the panic of a mother when her child is sick. They are in the stress of a business owner who just placed a major bid and then realizes or suspects he missed something. They are in the quiet reaches of our own souls every time we feel that maybe we haven't quite done enough in a given situation.

Here is what I told my author friend, and here is my advice to you. When you have a "Leave Everything To God Opportunity," realize that if you could do it alone, God wouldn't have made everyone else. Each of us has our own, unique experience that we bring to a situation. In short, each of us has a piece of the puzzle to fill in. As writers, we must realize that just because we couldn't see the piece that someone else lays before us, that doesn't mean we don't have skill, talent or desire, it just means that they have a different perspective, a different piece to fit into the mosaic of the work.

Instead of abhorring the pieces that someone else fills in, bless them. They just made your puzzle make more sense than it ever could have without that piece. Then thank God for bringing that piece into your life. When you begin to do that, you can then begin to slowly let go earlier and earlier in the process, and the puzzle can come together while you are building it rather than you having to knock it all apart and rebuild it later.

It's not easy for any of us to do, but when you think in terms of "Leave Everything To God Opportunities," the storms of life begin to look less frightening and more manageable than ever before. So try it today. Let Go, and see if He doesn't hand you a piece that on your own you couldn't have known or found but one that makes the whole puzzle fit in a way that it never could have without it. Then celebrate because you have now found the key to how God intended all of us to live, and that key will unlock doors you never imagined could open to you.

Let Go. Let God, and enjoy every "Leave Everything To God Opportunity" that comes your way.

(2004)

The Value of Honesty and Forgiveness

In watching *Star Wars III: Revenge of the Sith*, I came away with a very real sense of why honesty and forgiveness are so important to the Christian walk. In this movie, Anikan Skywalker is a bold, brash, headstrong young man who has more talent than wisdom, more stubbornness than patience. Through a series of events he makes some really bad decisions, decisions that weigh on his conscience with no way to get out.

There is a scene in the movie where Anikan, confused and distraught by the actions he has taken, goes to talk with Yoda. As they sit there across from one another, Anikan tries to explain the fear in his heart. He tries, but in reality he can't because that fear would necessarily preclude him from being on the Jedi Council, of which Yoda is a founding father and principle guide. So, he hedges the truth. He talks about the situations around him, wanting to go with his Jedi master to fight, wanting to protect the Republic, wanting to do the right thing but not knowing what that is.

However, his attempt at finding some peace in his tortured soul is doomed from the beginning. Why? Because Yoda cannot give him the thing he needs most—forgiveness. Even wise and powerful Yoda cannot remove himself from the situation and his own feelings of mistrust for the young man to really listen to what he is saying. You see, Yoda has his own agenda, his own allegiances, and in truth he has never trusted Anikan. This boy to whom much was given has abused that responsibility, and Yoda has no intention of helping him find his way back.

To me, this scene has a powerful message for any Christian willing to listen. We all do stupid things. We all mess up. In the fog of now, we all make dumb mistakes for which we are truly sorry, but if there is no outlet for that pain and no way to gain forgiveness for it, then we are irretrievably stuck in all the muck we've created in our lives.

This is the dichotomy laid out between the Old Testament and the New Testament. In the Old Testament, the people of Israel were really on their own. God gave them the Ten Commandments, which they couldn't really live up to, and said in effect, "Okay, here is what I expect. If you don't get it right, I will come and smite you down. Good luck." Talk about instilling fear of the Lord in you! In many churches today, this way of thinking still persists. You are ostensibly on a 24-hour surveillance by God, and He is sure to catch you doing something wrong. When He does, watch out!

And so, we became very good at rationalizing our sinfulness. We become very good at hiding what is really going on. We get very good at dressing ourselves up so we look like good, strong Christians on the outside—even if that isn't what's really going on. I heard a speaker once say that he grew up in the perfect church. No one sinned. They were all sick, but no one had lied to anybody, no one had anger in their heart. What he is saying is that, they couldn't confess who they really were (and get forgiveness for that) because if they confessed, they might well be judged unworthy by those they most needed forgiveness from—just like Anikan. So they had to live in those lies.

But God knew that we couldn't do it on our own. He knew we needed some way to say, "Hey, I messed up. Can you forgive me so I can let this go, stop torturing myself, and begin to live again?" In fact, you know His answer to this quandary: "For God so loved the world that He gave His only begotten Son that whosoever believeth in Him should not perish but have everlasting life."

Unlike learning the rules and trying to do it on your own, Christ gave us a new option. He said, "Come to Me all you who are weary and laden, and I will give you rest." He gave us a way to lay our burden of sin down. He gave us forgiveness. More than that, He gave us unconditional love. In other words, He taught us that the Father loves us no matter what we do. What a concept! He taught us it doesn't matter what we've done because God is greater than any sin we might ever have committed, and that we can come to the cross and lay that sin down, be forgiven, and walk away whole.

Anikan couldn't do that. The best he could do was talk around the truth of how much he needed forgiveness, how badly he hurt, how deeply confused he was. Like so many people in therapy, he talked around and around and around, but the hurt and the pain and the sins were still there. Now don't misunderstand me, there is a place for talking and getting things out. In fact, that is the first real lesson here—to have a place where you can be brutally honest about what's going on, to get all the muck out in the open.

But there is an undeniable second component as well, and that is to have someone on the listening end of that conversation who can offer forgiveness, or help you find forgiveness for yourself and others so that you can be released from the need to exact revenge on yourself for those sins.

Both components are found in the person of Jesus Christ. With Him you can be brutally honest. You can pour out every hurt and sadness and fear and wrong turn you've ever made, and He still loves you. In fact, His love for you never changes. It is the one constant in this world. And then after you have given Him the burden of your sins, He smiles gently and reminds you that you were forgiven 2000 years ago when He hung on that cross. It was and still is an indescribably wonderful gift, for what He has really given back to you is your life and your future because you no longer have to stay stuck in what you've done, you can now move on.

I wonder how many Anikans there are in the world—people walking around, wallowing in their guilt and shame with no place to lay that burden down. It is something to consider.

(2005)

8

On Words

For I am full of words, and the spirit within me compels me. –Job 32:18

In-Spir-Ation

I am a word nut. I think I have been forever. I even have a favorite and a least favorite letter of the alphabet. So basically, I'm a little weird. I love words. I love how by combining just 26 letters in a myriad of ways, I can take the pictures in my head and convey them to yours. To me, that's cool.

Many times I have found myself fascinated by a word that I have used forever but suddenly understand in a different light. So one day I was thinking of words and deconstructing them to see what they literally meant. I had gone through a couple when out of the blue the Holy Spirit said, "Yeah, it's like inspiration." I said, "What?" And He said, "It's like inspiration. Get it? In-spir-ation. Or literally being in the spirit."

Wow! I had been giving the Holy Spirit credit for my writing for a lot of years. Do you really think I could come up with the line "A lie doesn't understand truth anymore than fear understands faith"? No, way. That was totally from the Holy Spirit. However, I had been using the word inspiration like it just meant "uplifting" or "motivational."

What I had failed to see until that very moment was how being in-spir-ed literally meant one moment when you were in the Spirit – or more literally He was in you.

So the next time you feel inspired by something, give credit where credit is due and realize you have just had a visitor come into your life. Look around; it might be happening more than you think! (2004)

Decide

The genesis for my understanding of this word goes back to when I was teaching high school English. The school where I taught had a unique way to teach vocabulary. It was based entirely on learning the meanings of Greek and Latin root words. Now I have no idea how much that helped the kids, but it sure helped me.

When you deconstruct the word "Decide", you come up with two parts: de- and –cide. De means "away from" in Latin – as in destroy, devalue, detour, or diverge. Cid or cis means "to cut", as in incision.

Putting the two together, you get "to cut away from."

Now I had known this for a long time and always thought it fascinating. But it wasn't until I was talking with a friend of mine about a friend of hers that I realized how much understanding this could help others.

My friend was telling me how her friend just didn't get it. He refused to put things in God's Hands because he "didn't know how." I told her that what he (or anyone) has to do is to decide to do it – to put life in God's Hands. Then I said, "You know what decide means, right?'

That stopped her. No she didn't.

I deconstructed decide for her and then said, "To decide means to cut off all other possibilities." For example, let's say you decide to have hamburgers for supper. As soon as you decide, you literally cut yourself away from all other possibilities – brisket, sandwiches, steak, seafood. The others are now no longer options because you have decided to have hamburgers.

It works the same way in the spiritual realm although it's much less easy to see and therefore easier to let the important decisions slide.

Going to church, for instance. Have you ever really decided that church is beneficial for you – or do you just go because you're supposed to? How about having faith that the best outcome in God's eyes will happen? That's not an accident. It's a decision – where you literally cut yourself off from all other possibilities.

Deciding can be one of the most life-changing things you ever consciously do. It is like pruning a grapevine. If you let the vine go, it will be one big jumbled mess and produce very little fruit. But if you prune it, cutting away that which is simply in the way rather than productive, the good branches will have the room to produce richly.

So today when you make a decision about what to wear or how to spend your time, do it wisely and do it well for all the possibilities are available to you until the moment you decide. And once you decide, all the non-productive branches fall away – if you have decided wisely!

(2004)

De-Sire

Unfortunately for us, our culture can take even the most beautiful of things and turn them into ugly messes. Take the word "desire." I'm sure if you think of it, it conjures up all sorts of disgusting things – promiscuous sex, licentious living, pleasure and the pursuit of pleasure at any cost.

The problem with this is that it totally denigrates what the word desire really means. At its foundation it is a Spanish word. "De" means "of" and "sire" means "the Father." So the literal translation is "of the Father."

Therefore a desire is something "of the Father" – something God has given you. A desire is different than a want, which is more of yourself for yourself. It is also different than a need, for it goes beyond the basics of what it takes to live.

To me, God gave us desires to point us in the direction He wants us to go. If everyone tells you that you should be a computer analyst because they make a lot of money but your desire is to be a nurse, which do you listen to and why?

(2005)

L.I.G.H.T.

One of my Holy Spirit friends is teaching Sunday School to 7th grade girls this year. When she first started, my friend was a little lost as to what to teach and what other resources were available, so she innocently asked me if I could help. Little did either of us know where that one simple email would lead.

First, it was just figuring out what song she could use as an opener and then as a closer. I'm a music fanatic, so that wasn't too taxing. Then as the year progressed, we began working through what it means when things don't work out the way you thought they should. We discussed lessons—she is the consummate "activity guru," and I added in insights I've gleaned from my writing ministry. Together, we made a pretty good team.

Just after Christmas she came over to discuss her newest lesson. She had decided to do a lesson on the light of Christ coming into our world at Christmas. She had already gotten candles to use and everything. We worked out the activity— turning off the lights to start in darkness and then explaining with a single flame that Jesus came into our world and brought light. He gave His light to the early Christians, who passed it down through the generations to us, and now we have the opportunity to give His light to others.

The idea was that the first girl's candle would be lit from the Jesus candle, and then each girl would light the next girl's candle until all the candles were lit. We thought it was a pretty good plan—and then she got to class and had two girls instead of 14. She didn't do the light ceremony but did do the other activities she had planned to go with it.

When we talked again, she still wanted to do the light ceremony, but now she needed new activities. She told me that she was thinking about letting the girls take the word LIGHT and see what acronyms they could come up with. I agreed that it sounded like a good plan.

Then the Holy Spirit stepped in. Being a word freak and having some time on my hands as I drove to school to get my children, I started asking, "What would LIGHT stand for to me?"

I came up with some good ones: Love In God's Heart Today. Live In God's Hope Today. Then as I got closer to home, I looked down and noticed a fortune from a cookie we had gotten over the weekend lying on the seat next to me. I picked it up and read it. The word "Luck" jumped out at me because the book I am currently working on is called "Lucky."

Because I had been looking for "L" words, I immediately thought, "Hmm... Luck... How would that work in the word LIGHT?" Then a thought went through my head. "Luck Is God's Help." Instantly I got excited, but then I realized there was not a "T" word. So I said, "Okay, Holy Spirit but what does the T stand for?" Instantly the answer came... "Luck Is God's Help... Trusted."

You might think I came up with that. I didn't. It's too perfect. It's too Holy Spirit!

The cool thing is that for *years*—literally—people have told me that I was lucky. I always said, "Yeah, and I work darn hard to get that luck to work out." Up until the middle of last year, that was completely accurate in my life. I did work darn hard to be so "lucky." And it was work.

However, about the time my friend started teaching, I started putting things in the Holy Spirit's hands, and life has not been the same since. "Luck" has started literally pouring my direction. So much so, that when the title "Lucky" showed up for my new book, I knew it was perfect because the main theme is putting life in God's hands and how it works so much better when you do that.

Well, you can be sure that I couldn't wait to get home and call my friend. Thing is: *She called me first with awesome news!* (I love the way the Holy Spirit works!) Just before Christmas she had taken her teacher's certification test, and at the time she commented that it seemed that "everyone else is freaking out, but I'm not worried. I know whatever happens, it's what God meant to happen."

Then today she calls to tell me that she had gotten her scores in… A 91! 73 out of 80 questions right! That, for those of you who don't know, is a slam-dunk on a really challenging test!

Now some people might say she got lucky. But there's no doubt in my mind that she and I both know that "luck" came because she was living in the "light." Luck Is God's Help Trusted… It's such a cool way to live!

(2005)

Enthusiasm

Ever since reading *The Ragamuffin Gospel* by Brennan Manning, I have been having a lot of fun. Why? Because I let go of "I have to..." and started letting God dictate what went on the schedule for any given day. Let me tell you, that will open doors you never even knew were there.

A couple of my friends who are around me a lot caught the bug and began doing it too. And let me just say, life has never been more fun!

We get together now and talk Holy Spirit. We marvel at the things He puts in our lives to guide us, to encourage us, to teach us, or just to remind us He's there. Living that yourself is cool. Sharing it with others is the most awesome experience I've ever had.

To be able to pick up the phone and scream, "AHHH! You will never guess what the Holy Spirit did now!" is so incredible, it's hard to put into words.

Recently, I was reading a back issue of *O Magazine*, and I found this insight: the word enthusiasm, when translated from Greek means "with God." Talk about a grab-for-the-phone moment!

When I told one of my friends that, she said, "Oh, how true is that! The more I'm with God, the more excitement and fun comes into my life."

The other night, the same friend called. She had just gotten off work and was going to Wal-Mart. I could tell by the sound of her voice that it was not high on her want-to-do list. On a whim, (Thanks Holy Spirit) I said, "Smile at everyone there!"

Well let me tell you, by the time she got here after her shopping excursion, she was silly with fun. She said everyone she saw at Wal-Mart she gave a really big smile to. Apparently the reactions were worth the effort.

When I called her the next morning having just read the enthusiasm definition, she laughed. She knew exactly why... because living with God and sharing Him with the world can have no other effect than what we think of as "enthusiasm." I'll tell you what, those Greeks were smart people!

(2005)

References

I highly recommend each and every one of these sources as places to gain further inspiration!

Steve McVey, *Grace Rules*, (Harvest House Publishers, 1998).

Steve McVey, *Grace Walk*, (Harvest House Publishers, 2005).

Keith Urban, "Days Go By," *Be Here*. (Capitol Nashville, 2004).

Brennan Manning, *The Ragamuffin Gospel,* (Multnomah Publishers, 2000).

Casting Crowns, "Stained Glass Masquerade," *Lifesong*. (The Provident Group, 2005).

Bruce Wilkinson, *Secrets of the Vine*, (Multnomah Publishers, Inc. 2001).

Eugene H. Peterson, *The Message Bible/Remix,* (NavPress Publishing Group, 2003).

Marianne Williamson, *A Return to Love* (Harper Collins Publishers, 1992).

Og Mandino, *The Greatest Miracle in the World*, (Bantam Doubleday, 1983).

Bruce Wilkinson, *A Life God Rewards*, (Multnomah Publishers, Inc., 2002).

Keith Urban, "Song for Dad," *Golden Road*. (Capitol Nashville, 2002).

Staci Stallings, *Dreams by Starlight*, (Cyberserial at stacistallings.com, 2005).

Bob Dufford. *Be Not Afraid, (Hope Publishing Company).*

Anthony Robbins, *Awaken the Giant Within,* (Fireside; Simon & Shuster, 1992).

Sarah Ban Breathnach, *Something More,* (Warner Books, 1998).

Jean P. Sasson, *Princess*, (Avon Books, 1993).

LucasFilms, *Star Wars III: Revenge of the Sith*, (20th Century Fox, 2005).

Newmarket Films, *The Passion of the Christ*, (Newmarket Films, 2004).